FIRE IN THE BLOOD

Bad Witch Book 4

ROBYN BACHAR

FIRE IN THE BLOOD

Copyright © 2012 by Robyn Bachar

Robyn Bachar

P.O. Box 1692

Riverside IL 60546

Editing by Sue Ellen Gower

Cover by Kanaxa

❀ Created with Vellum

CONTENTS

Business was booming now that my competition was dead. Too booming. Over the years I'd wished many unfortunate things on the heads of my competitors, hoping that maybe one or two of them would get eaten by a demon, or promise one favor too many and get sucked into a hell dimension. Now I was the last surviving summoner west of Cincinnati and east of the Mississippi, and I'd never been so exhausted in my entire life. I needed a month at a tropical resort with a steady supply of drinks with little umbrellas in them to recover. Too bad the apocalypse was due any day now.

"Mistress, you haven't eaten today," Harvey commented from his spot on the couch in my office. My brow furrowed as I peered at him—I didn't feel hungry, and I was sure I'd eaten earlier.

"Yes, I did. I had that sub sandwich for lunch," I argued.

"No. That was yesterday." Harvey shook his head, his pointy ears twitching. The demon's bloodshot gaze was fixed on his tablet as it erupted with the cheeping of angry birds. I didn't understand his obsession with video games, but Harvey had been hooked ever since I first put a Gameboy into his skinless hands. I suspected it had something to do with the fact that pookas were elves once, and they shared the obsession that their faerie cousins had with games of chance. At least it kept him occupied while I did paperwork.

"It was?"

I opened my day planner and scanned my schedule. Damn. He was right. As an idiot teenager I'd traded my sense of taste for a favor from a lust demon—I was convinced that I was in love with a boy who ignored me, and that he would love me back if only he noticed me. Well, thanks to the demon he noticed me, and after a few sweaty sessions of bad sex in the backseat of his car, the boy noticed someone else. I was left with a broken heart, permanently numb taste buds and a stunted sense of smell. Hence, I forget to eat, because there's zero pleasure in it for me. This is why I'm skinny. It's not a lifestyle choice, a fitness obsession or anorexia. Most days I'm fueled solely by caffeine and bitchery, and with my new crazed schedule I was forgetting to eat more often than usual, because I didn't have time to eat. Or sleep. Or shower.

"Okay. Remind me to hit a drive-through on the way home."

"Are we leaving now?" he asked.

"Damn right we're leaving now," I muttered. It was almost midnight, and if we didn't escape soon, more calls would come in and I'd never get any sleep.

I saved the spreadsheet I'd been updating—half the work I was doing now didn't pay a single dime, which was putting a pinch on my income. Magiciankind was being hunted to extinction again, thanks to a government group of gun-toting fanatics and the demons pulling their strings. As the only summoner left, it was my job to stem the tide of invading demons. It was a good cause, and those never paid well. Then again, considering that said fanatics had wiped out my entire family along with the rest of the summoners, I would've done this job for free. Not that I was close with my family—I saw them on major holidays and the occasional birthday. I didn't miss them so far, because I didn't like most of them, but they didn't deserve to die. Vengeance wasn't normally my thing, but in this case, I was going to give it a shot.

The phone rang before I could get away from my desk. I glared at it as though my irritation could silence the ring, but then I swore as I recognized the number. It belonged to the Northern Illinois Paranormal Society—a group of straights who hunt ghosts, they're adorable—and they only call me when something bad has happened.

"All on Red Consulting, Patience speaking," I said as I picked up the phone.

"Ms. Roberts, it's Dan Pulaski. Do you have a moment?"

A chorus of avian cheering drew my attention and I pointed threateningly at Harvey until he muted his game. "Sure. What's up?"

Dan was the head of their group, a Chicago firefighter by day and ghost hunter by night. I liked him. He was cute, but being descended from a clan of fire faeries, I wouldn't consider dating someone who suppressed fire instead of starting it. The fact that he wasn't a magician was also a deal breaker.

"One of our investigators was pushed down a flight of stairs. He broke his leg."

My desk chair squeaked as I leaned back. Straights could be excitable when it came to investigating supposed supernatural events, so it could be the man simply tripped. "You're certain he was pushed?"

"Yeah, I was with him. I heard a growl before it happened, and there was a bad smell. Plus it looks like he has scratches on his chest where he says the hand pushed him."

I scowled—so much for sleep. That was demonic activity, and we both knew it. For the most part, NIPS is a harmless group of hobbyists. Though they're very common, ghosts are pretty low on the paranormal totem pole, because they're selfish bastards focused on their own drama for all eternity and only necromancers can interact with them. Ghosts can't physically interact with the world of the living, and moving objects and slamming doors are usually the result of demonic activity. (Sometimes it's faeries with nothing better to do, but that's rare.) This is why NIPS calls me, because demons are summoner territory. They don't know what I am, but somewhere along the line they'd heard from a friend who'd heard from a friend that I was a "demonologist"—as I said, they're adorable—and that's how we met.

"What's your location? Business or residence?" I asked.

"Residence. The family's here, if you want to interview them."

Family. Shit. Here I thought I could tell NIPS to go home and I'd add it to my To-Do List, but not with a family involved. "Yes, I do."

Dan thanked me, and I jotted the address down and promised I'd be there soon. It was in Wrigleyville, which wasn't too far from my office. Traffic would be light at this late hour, and because it was November I didn't have any Cub games to contend with for parking.

"You still haven't eaten," Harvey reminded after I hung up the phone.

"Drive through. Don't let me forget."

"You said that this morning."

"I did?" I asked in surprise.

"Yes, you did."

Damn it all to hell and back, my brain must really be fried, because I had zero memory of that. At least I'd been chugging black coffee all day, so there was something in my system, even if it was only caffeine. I couldn't keep this pace up for much longer, but I didn't have a choice. I was the only one left to handle the demon problem. I'd tried to call in extra help from the coasts, and everyone turned me down. They were too afraid of the hunters, and though I couldn't blame them for that, it still pissed me off. I outsourced what work I could to the local guardians, but it wasn't enough. They weren't specialists like me.

I was trying to bail out the *Titanic* with a teaspoon. It was only a matter of time before we all drowned.

"Well, this time I mean it," I said lamely.

"Of course, Mistress."

I grabbed my black cashmere coat from the rack and donned it along with my scarf, then slung my messenger bag over my shoulder. This time I made it halfway across the room before I was stopped, but it wasn't the phone that interrupted me. It was a faerie invasion, and I had only a moment to recognize Faust by the smoky lenses of his round, dark glasses before he pounced on me. He kissed me fiercely and nudged me back until I stumbled into the front of my desk.

"I dislike this overcoat. It's much too bulky." He reached for the buttons and I batted his hand away.

"I'll be in the car, Mistress," Harvey called out loudly before vanishing. He's not a voyeur, and he disapproved of my relationship with Faust. I didn't approve of my relationship with Faust either. Every summoner knows you shouldn't fuck a faerie, because it always ends bad.

"Cut it out. I'm on a call," I warned.

Faust grinned, and my chest tightened with an emotion I fought not to show. Yes, this was headed toward disaster, but I couldn't help myself. Faust was the most addictive temptation I'd ever met. He was tall for a faerie, which made him about my height, and dark haired with a pale complexion that spoke more of a vampire than a faerie. Faust had an angular face with high, sharp cheekbones that reminded me a bit of a runway model, a finely-drawn brow and a smile that could make a girl weak in the knees in 0.5 seconds.

"It can't wait," he insisted. "I've missed you."

He tugged my scarf aside and kissed my neck, and it was suddenly much too warm to be wearing my coat. I didn't fight him as he unbuttoned the garment and slid it off. I kissed him and indulged in the lovely diversion of letting his nimble hands roam for a few moments, because the past few days had been all business and no pleasure. But I had an appointment to keep, and I pushed him away with a disappointed sigh.

"I missed you too, babe, but I don't have time for a break. I'm on call 24/7 now."

"I know you are." Faust's expression sobered, and he caressed my cheek. "You're a brave woman, Patience, and I admire that about you. But that's also why I'm here."

"You're here because you admire me? Funny, seemed more like desire a second ago," I teased. The corners of his mouth twitched, and I bit back the urge to kiss him. Experience had taught me that if I encouraged him I'd end up naked and bent over the desk.

"There's a problem—" he began, and I cut him off.

"I don't have time for more problems. We're all full up here."

"This is serious. Zachary has hired someone to kill you."

Zachary Harrison was a billionaire vampire and arguably one of the most powerful magicians in the country, aside from myself. My empty stomach twisted, and for a moment the fear that Faust had come to do the job himself slithered through my veins. After all, he worked for Harrison, and he was a shadowspawn faerie. Faust's entire clan had been banished from Faerie for doing unspeakable acts of evil. Normally his past didn't bother me, because as a summoner I could spot evil at fifty paces and he didn't set off any of my alarms. I assumed while the rest of his family might be guilty, he'd been falsely accused. Then my good sense kicked in and reminded me that Faust wouldn't hurt me. I trusted him, which for me was a really big deal. I don't trust easily.

I cleared my throat and squared my shoulders. "Well he'll have to get in line. I assume he's pissed because I helped the Titania?"

"Quite."

Damn it, I knew that was going to come back and bite me in the ass. I should've said no, but being faerie-blooded, I couldn't refuse an order from the Titania and Oberon. They'd needed a ritual from the shadow realm—a ritual that freed the Titania from being bound to Harrison—and I helped them retrieve it.

"Why come at *me*? I'm not the only one who ruined his evil plans. It was a group effort," I pointed out.

"As I understand it, he is targeting several people for his revenge in this matter."

"Of course he is. Go warn the Titania and she'll put a stop to it.

I'm running late." I picked up my coat and started for the door again, and he grabbed my arm.

"This is serious. He's become...unstable since the bond between him and the Titania was broken. I believe it had unexpected side effects, and it's growing worse. He isn't listening to me, and he won't listen to her. Not about this. He will see you dead."

"Then tell the pretty boy to take his best shot. I'm not afraid of him. Look, I appreciate the heads up, but it doesn't change anything. I still have work to do. If I hid every time someone threatened to kill me I'd never leave the house," I joked, but Faust didn't appear amused.

He calmly removed his glasses, revealing the pale blue eyes that I'd only seen a few times before. I don't know why he hides them, because he doesn't have a pressing reason like I do. His eyes are so light they're almost clear, but blue is a nice, normal color, unlike yellow. As though hearing my internal monologue, he pulled my sunglasses off next and set them on the desktop. I hoped my eyes weren't glowing. I hate it when that happens.

Faust stared at me with a seriousness I don't often see from him. Our relationship is built on lust, and we have an understanding that we enjoy each other's company without mentioning commitment or the future. Really, a future isn't possible with a faerie lover, because he'll live forever and I have an expiration date. Faust slid his arms around me and held me close, and I fought to appear unaffected as my pulse leapt.

"Patience, please listen to me. You're one of the strongest magicians I've ever had the pleasure of knowing, but you're exhausted. You're doing work that should be handled by dozens of summoners. There are hunters, demons and powers know what else out there trying to kill you, and now Zachary's hired a master necromancer as well. It's only a matter of time before you make a mistake."

"I don't make mistakes," I argued sullenly. It was an outright lie, but you don't become a cast-iron bitch by admitting your weaknesses.

He smiled. "Of course. Take the rest of the night off. Come home with me. I'll make you dinner, and you can get some sleep."

My brow rose. I didn't know he had a place of his own. Most of our horizontal activity occurred in my office, with the occasional late-night booty call at my condo. "That's a nice offer, and I'll happily take a rain check, but right now I have plans."

"Then let me come with you. I'll watch your back while you work."

Stepping away to get some thinking distance, I ran my fingers through my hair as I considered it. I needed a haircut, though I doubted I'd fit one in before the apocalypse started. What started out as a trendy, angular cut had grown into a messy mop. My fire-engine-red hair was something I'd been born with thanks to my faerie blood. It's a shade that doesn't naturally occur in humans. In the past it would've marked me as abnormal, and I might've been killed by a mob of superstitious villagers with torches and pitch-forks, but in the modern age I could claim it was an unfortunate dye job.

Not that any of that aside helped me figure out what to do about Faust, who was still watching me far too intently. This was odd behavior, even for him. The cold, dark part of my soul that'd been corrupted by dozens of deals with demons whispered that I should tell him to get the fuck out and never come back, because I didn't need him. I didn't need anyone. I choked the urge down like a mouthful of bad medicine.

"Why?" I asked. "Don't get me wrong, I'm grateful, but why warn me? You're on Harrison's payroll. Shouldn't your loyalty be to him?"

He frowned. "No, not for this. I love you."

I froze as the world paused around me, because that was not the answer I was expecting. I'd heard him speak those words often enough in my dreams—and occasionally in my nightmares—but I never thought I'd hear them in reality. My heart leapt at the idea and then plummeted at the sheer insanity of it.

"Don't say that," I muttered as I rubbed my face with my hands.

"Do you doubt my affection for you?" he asked, sounding offended.

"No."

And that was part of the problem. I knew he was sincere, but there was zero potential for happily ever after with a faerie, no matter how badly I might want it. I'd known that going into the affair. Gripped by the sudden craving for a smoke, I dropped my coat on my desk and walked back behind it to rifle through the top drawer. After some searching I found a pack of cloves and withdrew a black cigarette. I lit the end with my fingertips—I love being descended from a fire faerie.

Faust continued to study me, and I shivered as I inhaled. "Are you going to deny having feelings for me?" he asked.

Lie to him. Now both my good sense and my bad sense screamed it at me. Deny everything. Tell him he was nothing more than a good fuck. End it now before it went any further...but I couldn't. I don't often have squishy moments, and *vulnerable* is a word that's never been used to describe me, but I couldn't lie to Faust. I'd been doing my best to keep my feelings bottled up and hidden for months, because I figured sooner or later he'd move on to a new obsession, and I wanted to be prepared for it when he did. Faeries are wanderers, and they don't stick to one lover for long. We'd been fooling around for almost three years, and I'd feared that the end would come any day now.

Apparently not. Of course, that was part of the problem—I was used to people leaving. I never expected anything permanent from anyone, but Faust had stayed with me far longer than any other lover I'd had.

"That's not the point," I said.

"So you do love me."

"That's not what I said. There's no future in this. We're not even the same species. You're Peter Pan, and I'm Wendy. You'll still be a lost boy when I'm old and gray."

He stepped closer, extending a hand to take mine. "That doesn't matter—"

"Hell yes it matters!" I shouted as I flinched away. "It matters to me. I'm sure plenty of girls have fallen for the *love is the only thing that matters* speech, but not this one. I don't need you to be my knight in shining armor. I take care of myself. I always have."

He sighed. "I know you do. I'm not saying you can't protect yourself. I'm only suggesting that you allow me to share the burden for the time being."

My mouth twitched as I fought the urge to grin. He did have a way with words. "No. If you want to help, then go tell the Oberon about Harrison's plans for me, and remind Duquesne that he's still contractually obligated to have my back. I'd hate to call in that favor this soon, but I'll do it if I have to."

"Very well." He didn't look pleased, but it'd get him off my case for now. Faust vanished, and I finished my cigarette in silence.

This was bad on so many levels. I was used to people wanting to kill me, because I'd received my first death threat at seventeen. Life as a summoner meant that I dealt with a lot of bad people, but an amorous faerie declaring his love for me...Lord and Lady, that was a problem I hadn't been expecting. I'd rather deal with an incubus, because at least they were straightforward about what they wanted. I mentally kicked myself again for getting involved with Faust. It was the charm that wore me down. He'd shown up at my door with work from Zachary Harrison, and after a few meetings we started mixing business with pleasure.

That was a mistake I'd never make again. If he was a summoner it'd be different—I might've even pinned him down and demanded marriage and babies, the whole domestic package. It was an option I considered for my retirement, but I'd never had a relationship with another summoner last more than a month. Once I had one of the west coast councilmen propose the idea of "breeding" with me. Completely unromantic—sure, I've been called a bitch more times than I can count, but that doesn't mean I'd sign up to be a summoner puppy mill—but he did have a point that we would have exceptionally powerful offspring. I might have even seriously considered it if he'd agreed to artificial insemination, but he wanted to do it the old-fashioned way, and the guy was so creepy he made my skin crawl, so that was a definite no.

I didn't have that problem with Faust. I loved him. Visions of chubby babies with bright red hair and pale blue eyes danced in my head. With a growl I ground out my cigarette in the ashtray, grabbed my specs and my coat and hurried out of my office before something else could go wrong. It had been a long day, and I had a feeling it was going to be an equally long night.

I really needed that vacation.

CHAPTER TWO

Harvey had hounded me until I found a twenty-four-hour drive through, and I scarfed down two chicken sandwiches and a few handfuls of fries on the way to the NIPS investigation. Not my finest hour, but it resembled food closely enough that I wouldn't pass out from hunger. Exhaustion was sure to get me first.

I don't often visit Wrigleyville in the fall. It's rare that the Cubs make it to post-season play, so by October I've moved on to watching the Bears. The area felt emptier without the noise from the sea of drunk Cub fans. Thankfully it also made traffic lighter and parking easier. My GPS guided me to the location of the NIPS investigation, but spotting them was fairly obvious thanks to their "command center" van parked in front of the house and the group of people milling about in matching hooded sweatshirts. I had to admit, their logo was cute—a cartoon ghost with its tail being tugged on by a German shepherd puppy. I parked behind the van, grabbed my bag and hopped out of my car.

"Ms. Roberts," Dan greeted. I nodded up at him—he was tall and broad-shouldered, and I suspected he'd played football in college. Maybe if I'd jumped him when I had the chance I wouldn't have my lovesick faerie predicament. But then again, relationships with the non-magical majority never work out well. Summoner relationships in general rarely work out well. We're a selfish, cutthroat bunch of bastards.

"Mr. Pulaski. Send your team home," I ordered, and he scowled.

"There's still time left to investigate."

"Not tonight. Didn't you say one of your buddies broke a leg?"

Dan winced. "Yes."

"And, what, you're hoping someone will break their neck next? It's not safe in there. Besides, there won't be anything left to investigate when I'm done, so they might as well call it a night."

Dan sighed, but then he nodded. "All right, but Andy and I are staying until you're done."

"That's fine."

I figured as much. Dan and his brother Andy were the founding members of NIPS, and they were always willing to go the extra mile for an investigation. Part of me wanted to warn them off, worried that one night they'd encounter a real danger and get seriously hurt—or dead—but I knew they'd only dig in deeper if I did. They were on a quest for knowledge about the supernatural, armed with digital recorders and thermal cameras. Being supernatural myself, I understood that the things that go bump in the night kill without remorse, and they know all the best ways to dispose of a busybody's corpse.

"Come on. The family's inside. I'll introduce you," he said.

Harvey followed me as I followed Dan. The straights can't see Harvey. Most magicians can't even see Harvey—it's one of his talents. It's useful having backup that no one knows is there, and he's saved my ass on more than one occasion. Most summoners at my skill level have several servants, but he's the only being I've ever permanently bound to me. I don't play well with others, and having more than one servant just seemed gratuitous. Plus Harvey's gaming habit eats up enough of my petty cash.

The family huddled together in the front room, comprised of Mom, Dad and two daughters—a very normal-looking, all-American bunch. The youngest was asleep on the loveseat, bundled under a quilt, but it was the older girl who caught my attention. Teenager. Figures. Teenage girls are going to be the death of us all one day.

"Mr. and Mrs. Sanders, this is Ms. Roberts. She's a specialist."

The teenager squirmed beneath my regard. People find my specs unnerving, but they'd find my eyes far more disturbing so I keep the glasses on.

"Where's the Ouija board?" I asked.

"Pardon?" the mom said. I bet she had no idea what her daughter brought into the house.

"Where. Is. The Ouija board?" I repeated. My voice rose, and the girl flinched as her eyes widened.

"How did you know?"

"Angry spirits don't show up without an invitation, kiddo. Using a Ouija board is like chumming the water for sharks."

Which was, unfortunately, true, though spirits of the dead had nothing to do with it. What started as a clever summoner scheme for luring unsuspecting demons into this world to be bound as servants ended up as a mass-produced party game. It's not magic, not in the usual sense, but it's a tool. Using a Ouija board doesn't make a straight a magician, but it does give them a party line to the hell dimensions. You never know who might pick up, and I spent a lot of time tracking down strays drawn to suburbia by girls at slumber parties. The problem had gotten worse since the summoner population had decreased to just me.

Mr. Sanders looked skeptical. "It's just a game."

"Only it's not. Did the activity start after you brought it into the house?" I asked. The girl pondered it for a moment, and then nodded. "Well there you go. So where is it?"

"Under my bed."

I glanced at Harvey, and he left to take care of it. There'd be nothing left of the thing except for a layer of ash when he was done. Good riddance. I fucking hate Ouija boards. One of these days I was going to find the Parker Brothers and end them, provided the apocalypse didn't do it first.

"I'm going to need everyone out of the house while I clear it. I suggest a hotel room if you don't have friends or family nearby. This might take a while."

The father began to argue, but was interrupted by the low bass rumble of a growl that shook the glass trinkets in the curio cabinet. I blinked, startled. That wasn't Harvey—sometimes I'd have him pull a few parlor tricks if the straights argued with me, but only when I gave the order. It was a bad sign. Time to eject the family so I could get down to business.

"Here," I reached into my jacket and withdrew my money clip. "This should cover your expenses, and any damages." I peeled off a few hundreds and pressed them into the father's hand.

"Damages?" he repeated. Another growl knocked a photo from the wall behind them, and the glass shattered in the frame when it hit the floor. Okay, very bad sign. The sudden local summoner extinction meant that bigger, meaner demons were slipping through the wards.

"Everybody out," I ordered.

The family hustled, spurred on by more ominous growling. Dan frowned as he turned to me. "Do you want my help?"

"No." The word was almost a snarl, and I paused as his brow rose. "Sorry. Long day. You and Andy can stay out front until I give the all clear, if you want."

"All right. Good luck."

He followed the family out—the man was good with orders, I'd give him that. I waited until the count of ten before shucking my coat and tossing it on the couch, followed by my suit jacket. I rolled up the sleeves of my blouse, and the steady beat of approaching footsteps caught my attention as I fished through my bag for my bottle of salt.

"How bad is it, Harv?" I asked without looking up.

"There appears to be a demon infestation in this house," Faust replied. I jumped, spilling spell components across the living room floor. He stood in the doorway, his hands neatly folded in front of him, calm and serene while my heart revved to one hundred miles an hour.

"Lord and Lady, don't *do* that," I sputtered. "You're supposed to be talking to the Oberon."

"I did. He asked that I keep an eye on you in the meantime, so here I am, at his request." He smiled his Cheshire cat grin, and I sighed. If I kicked him out I'd piss off the Oberon, which I couldn't afford to do at the moment. Duquesne was still harboring ill will toward me because I'd stabbed him once, despite the fact that he'd deserved it. Some people just can't let things go.

"All right, fine. Just stay out of the way." Irritated, I snatched up the supplies and tossed them back into the bag. Faust nodded, and then kissed me quickly. "Cut it out, I'm on the clock," I warned him with a sharp poke to his ribs.

"Of course." He scowled a bit, but he followed as I went in search of Harvey.

True to form, the NIPS investigators had turned off all the lights in the building. They seem to think that darkness helps paranormal activity, but that's not true. The magical world works 24/7/365, rather like me lately. But I left the lights off, hoping to prevent the impending throw-down from being spotted from outside, or worse, caught on one of their cameras. I paused in the hallway to put my specs in their case in my bag, and then withdrew my police brutality model flashlight. Not that I needed it to see in the dark with my special eyes, but the flashlight kept up the illusion of being normal and gave me a lovely bludgeoning weapon to bash a demon in the head with.

Harvey peered past me and twitched his spindly ears in irritation at Faust. "Mistress, I thought you dismissed your lover for the evening." He sounded a little whiny, but it was hard to tell, because his voice was difficult to read. Pookas are different from most demons, because they were made demons, not born that way. When the elves were about to become extinct, a group of pookas made a deal with a demon to save their lives, not knowing that the price of their "salvation" was permanent demonhood—a lesson in being careful what you wish for.

I snorted. As if it was that easy to be rid of Faust...well, it would be, if I knew his True Name, but no such luck there. "Play nice, boys. Did you 86 the Ouija board?"

"Yes, Mistress."

"Good." At least one thing had gone right. "Did you spot our troublemaker?"

Harvey shot a meaningful glance at Faust before replying. "I spotted an envy demon that appears to be the source of the growling theatrics. There is, however, a stronger presence I have not identified yet."

"We'll bag the small fry and work our way up then," I said.

I worked my way through each room of the house with my entourage behind me. The air was charged and heavy, at odds with the bland surroundings. There were a few personal touches here and there, but otherwise it looked like every other family home I'd seen. With my colorful upbringing, I had little experience with what the average home was like, so walking through one made me feel like a stranger in a strange land. The simple trappings of dolls and pop band posters were foreign to me. Normal families don't sacrifice small animals at holidays, right?

On my first pass I warded the doors and windows, ensuring that the uninvited guests stayed in and couldn't escape. The growling increased in protest, and I didn't like that one bit. Almost all demons are a pain to banish, but envy demons are particularly stubborn buggers. Like beautiful, unique snowflakes, demons come in more varieties than can easily be counted, because there are several hells. Some demons take after sins and vices, some stick to elements like fire and ice, and some are just fucking scary bogeymen from our worst nightmares.

Because I had extra backup, I sent Harvey outside to keep an eye on the NIPS brothers and make sure they weren't trying to film me. We had an agreement that they stayed out of my way and didn't record any of my work, but though I liked them, I didn't trust them, and I didn't want to end up on YouTube.

I cornered the vociferous demon in the teenager's bedroom, which I assumed was where the bastard had gotten into the house in the first place. The closet doors shook with another warning growl, and after I stowed my flashlight my hands burst into flame with a soothing tingle of magic. Fire magic typically falls into sorcerer territory, but thanks to my faerie lineage it's one of my special skills.

"Look, we can do this easy, or we can do this the hard way, but you're going to be evicted," I warned.

The doors exploded outward as something the size of a Rottweiler launched itself at me. My breath rushed from my lungs as it knocked me down and started for the door, but Faust blocked its exit. This time I tackled the bugger, and it howled as I grabbed its hind legs. Greasy dark green fur singed at my touch, and it turned and snapped at me with a mouth filled with shark's teeth. I held tight and spat the words of a simple banishing spell, but nothing happened.

The demon took the opportunity of my failure to sink its teeth into my arm. Sharp pain lanced through it as the demon shook its head back and forth, digging in deeper, and I swallowed a scream. As I started a second, more powerful banishing spell a flaming sword appeared in Faust's hand—neat trick, that—and he stabbed the demon in the chest. The second spell worked, and the demon vanished with a wail and a hint of smoke. I doused my hands before I accidentally lit the carpet on fire.

"Let me see," Faust insisted. He knelt next to me and examined the wound. My forearm was a bleeding mass of raw meat. It hurt like hell, but I sternly reminded myself that I'd had worse, and I couldn't afford to panic. "I'm not adept at healing."

"Bathroom. I'll clean it in the sink and wrap it," I said.

My heart raced from the adrenaline and I trembled a bit, but I got to my feet and hustled out of the room. With my good hand I flipped the lights on and blinked at the yellow décor. Who paints a bathroom yellow, honestly? Blood dripped on the tile floor, and I hurried to the sink and stuck my forearm under a stream of cold water. Lord and Lady, it looked bad. My stomach heaved, and I snarled another string of expletives before nodding to my bag.

"I've got healing potions and bandages in there," I said.

"Does this happen often?" Faust pulled the bag's flap up and searched through the contents. He stood close, and I indulged in resting my head on his shoulder for a moment.

"Often enough. I swear they're getting bitchier the past few days. Most go without a fight once they realize they're cornered."

"Perhaps I should handle the next one," he suggested.

"You can banish demons?" Any magician can handle a mild to average demon, provided they know the basics of what to do. Faust wasn't technically a magician though—faeries are magic itself.

"Of course." He handed me a plastic bottle filled with a healing potion, and I popped the top and chugged it down. Cool magic spread through me, and the deep tears in my flesh knitted together. The potion wasn't powerful enough to completely mend it, but it closed the worst of it and slowed the bleeding to a manageable trickle instead of a stream.

I breathed a sigh of relief, and I didn't argue with Faust when he took the liberty of bandaging my arm. "Well, when we find the second one, you're welcome to try to banish it."

"Perhaps you should wait here while I take care of it," he suggested.

"I'm not that injured."

"You nearly lost an arm."

I rolled my eyes. "Please, it's only a flesh wound. That's good enough for now."

My arm tingled as I flexed my fingers, but I could deal with it. I had stronger healing potions at home for emergencies, though I hoped I wouldn't need them. I cleaned up the blood trail with a hand towel—the money for damages I'd given the dad would cover a new set of bath towels—and tossed it into the sink.

One down, one to go. The second demon was a sneaky bastard. I sensed its presence like a spike of magic stabbing me behind the eyes in a summoner's migraine, but I couldn't pinpoint his whereabouts. As we checked through the house I caught a few flashes of movement out of the corner of my eyes, but the figure vanished the moment I turned toward it.

"I don't like this," I said as I paused outside the master bedroom.

"What's wrong?" Faust asked.

"I hate this cat-and-mouse bullshit."

"Are you the cat or the mouse?" he teased.

I turned and pointed at him to warn him that I was not amused, but when I did I spotted a shadow standing behind him. "Get down!" I shouted.

Faust ducked as ordered, and I hurled a handful of fire at the shadow. It dodged to the side and dove through the doorway to the master bedroom.

"It's a shadow demon," I warned. Rare for one to have slipped into a family residence, because they prefer abandoned buildings where they can roam freely in the dark.

"Understood."

Faust stepped into the room, and when I followed I slapped on the lights. I blinked for a moment, but the more light there was, the fewer places the shadow demon would have to hide in. The room was empty, and I frowned.

"Hello, Patience," a voice said from behind me.

Before I could turn I was yanked back and thrown down a flight of stairs. I crashed to the floor at the bottom in a heap of tangled limbs and indignation. My shoulder screeched in protest as I sorted myself out. Dislocated. Shit.

Faust appeared at my side. "Are you hurt?"

"Yes. Where'd he go?"

"I didn't see."

"Fine. Help me up. And pop my shoulder back in if you can."

He helped me to my feet and then relocated my shoulder as

requested. This time I did scream, but I felt it was warranted considering the amount of holy-shit pain it caused. Afterward Faust held me close. The comfort was nice, but I spotted the shadow demon behind him, standing in the middle of the living room. I tensed, and Faust whirled, his fiery sword reappearing in his hand.

The demon titled its head to the side as it regarded us. "So Patience Roberts has a sweetheart. How quaint."

"Kris?" I questioned. The voice sounded like Kris, but it couldn't be. Kristoff Valkyrie was an ancient shadow demon, and ancient demons didn't travel to earth. They couldn't.

"In the flesh, as it were," he replied. The demon smiled his dark grin. As a shadow demon, he was made of darkness from head to foot, and he moved with fluid, languid motions as though walking through water.

"That's not possible." I shook my head, and a trickle of blood slid down the side of my face. Guess I hit my head when I fell. Maybe I was hallucinating, because that was the only way this made sense.

"And yet here I am." Kris stepped closer, and I flinched as Faust growled at him.

"Keep your distance," Faust said.

I swallowed hard. I couldn't banish an ancient demon. No one could. There just wasn't a spell for it, because no one had ever needed one. I also couldn't kill the bastard, because you can't kill a demon on Earth, only banish them back where they came from. We were pretty much fucked, but I wasn't about to go without a fight.

"And why are you here? I never pegged you as a voyeur, or a pedophile," I said.

Kris hissed, apparently offended. "I came to see you, Patience. I did tell you that we would see each other again."

"Next time, feel free to send an email instead."

The demon smiled and stepped toward me, and Faust raised his weapon.

"You'll not touch her," he warned. I had a moment of warm fuzzies. He was defending me. That was a first for me.

"Go get him, babe," I encouraged. Not because I needed defending, but he'd make a great distraction for what I planned to do next. Faust leapt at Kris, and they became a blur of shadow and flames.

First I unwove the ward blocking the front windows. I couldn't send the bastard back to the shadow realm, but I could evict him from the premises. Glass shattered and wood splintered as the shadowspawn faerie versus ancient demon rumble raged in the living room. I knelt on the shag carpet and dug through my bag, grabbing salt and water and other summoner trinkets. Witches and alchemists are better known for needing spell components, but we're almost as bad. I drew a rough circle with the salt and began chanting in Latin, casting the biggest warding spell I could manage on the fly.

"Don't you dare," Kris snarled at me.

I paused between verses to warn Faust to get down, and with the final words of the spell the magic flared and exploded. The shockwave hurled Kris out the front windows, raining glass across the lawn, and I lurched forward and warded the empty space. Kris tumbled over the grass, and then he disintegrated, off to haunt somewhere else for now. Probably to Gary. Demons love Gary, Indiana. It was a temporary solution, but hopefully it would give me a few hours to breathe—or better yet, to sleep.

"Are you all right?" Faust asked.

Nodding, I glanced up at him. A trio of slashes marred his face, and blood oozed from the wounds. The blood was a reminder that faeries are ageless, but not immortal. He could be killed, especially by something as powerful as an ancient demon, and the fear of it grabbed my chest and squeezed with icy fingers.

"Yes. Are you?" I blurted. I touched his face, and he smiled reassuringly as the wounds healed and vanished without a trace.

"It's only a scratch. Is your work here finished? I would like to take you home."

I laughed dryly, because with Kris involved my work was really just starting, but I nodded. "Yes, for now. Let me settle up with the straights and we can go."

I hoped that the NIPS boys hadn't recorded that, because I had no idea how to explain it, and I didn't want to have to threaten to break their legs if they didn't delete it. Harvey appeared at my side, his ears twitching in disapproval as he glared at Faust.

"Mistress, was that Kristoff Valkyrie?" Harvey asked.

"Yes it was," I replied.

"How bothersome."

That was Harvey, king of understatements. I fished my specs out of my bag and started combing through the chaos for my coat. "Just go wait in the car," I ordered. "I need to stop Dan and Andy before they tweet about this."

CHAPTER THREE

"I'd really rather just go home. To my home," I repeated as I pulled into the parking garage. At this point I was just being whiney, but I couldn't help it. I'd had a bad night—a series of bad nights, thanks to the demon invasion.

"I know, but your place isn't safe." Faust rubbed my knee in what I assumed was meant to be a comforting gesture, but it sent my mind spinning in another direction, specifically of the conversation we'd had in my office earlier. I didn't want to continue that conversation. "You can park there. It's one of my spaces."

"One of? How many do you have?" I asked.

"Three. I keep one open for guests."

Parking spots are prime real estate in the city. I only have one spot at my condo, and I pondered adding more as I pulled my car into the spot.

"May I stay here, Mistress?" Harvey asked from the backseat.

"Here? In the garage? Really?" I asked, surprised.

"I would rather not be in the area should you and your lover become amorous."

I sighed. I didn't think that was on the menu, considering how injured I was at the moment. My tumble down the stairs had turned me into a walking bruise.

Faust turned and peered back at the demon. "I have a guest room. You're welcome to it."

"I don't get the guest room?" I asked.

"No, you don't," he replied simply.

Or maybe sex was on the menu after all. Staying with Faust was a terrible idea, but with Kristoff Valkyrie and an unknown vampire assassin gunning for me, I needed all the help I could get. Having Faust on my side was in my best interest. Besides, I was pretty sure said vampire assassin was at my place right that moment, probably perusing my movie collection or nosing through my underwear drawer.

"Harvey gets the guest room. We'll try to keep the volume down," I promised.

My demon didn't seem pleased by the idea, but he followed as we took the elevator up into the building. A Zachary Harrison-owned building, I noted from the signage around the place. I wondered if Harrison knew about Faust and me. I hoped not. I didn't want to get into another brawl if there was a vampire waiting to pounce in Faust's place. The elevator brought us up to the penthouse—of course, nothing but the best for the associates of Zachary Harrison. He was rich, famous, powerful, handsome, and he gave me the creeps. Unlike Faust, he pinged my evil radar, which was why I kept our visits to a minimum even before he put a hit out on me.

I eyed the décor while Faust showed Harvey to the guest room. It was surprisingly bland and conservative for a faerie's home, because they're usually into bling and bold colors. The place was bigger than my condo, but I tied up a lot of my money in investments and savings instead of luxury. If I lived long enough to retire, I'd be a millionaire when I did. Judging by the size, I was willing to bet there was more than one guest room in a place this big, but I didn't call Faust on it. Yet. It would depend on how our conversation went.

I went in search of the kitchen, and more importantly, of a cold beverage. A glass of wine would be nice, but I was just plain thirsty and I'd settle for anything. Food would also be helpful after my trip down the stairs. I opened the cabinets, looking for a water glass, but the shelves were empty. No food, no dishes. The fridge was empty too, but then again my fridge was pretty bare. I collected condiments, soda and expired take-out. Poor Harvey was very tired of me asking him to smell things to see if they'd gone bad.

"Here. Try this," Faust said from behind me.

I turned and he offered me a plain white coffee mug of pink drink, the faerie version of a medicinal energy drink. It'd cure all my aches, pains, cuts and bruises—hell, it could probably bring me back from the dead.

"I'm not hurt that bad," I protested.

"You need your strength." He smiled, and I peered at him warily.

"Why, what do you have planned?"

His grin widened, and I walked away to sit on a stool next to the kitchen island. I sipped the drink and wondered what it tasted like. Delicious, probably. I missed delicious, it was a distant memory. Healing magic tingled from my lips to my toes and back in a prickly wave.

"You have history with this shadow demon?" Faust asked.

"Kris? We go way back, and I'm not his favorite person. Look, I know you're wound up about Harrison's hired killer, but this is worse. Kris is an ancient demon. He shouldn't be able to get through to this world, and now that he's here, I'm not sure I can send him back. It's never happened before that I know of. I sure as hell don't have a spell that'll banish him."

Faust tilted his head to the side and stroked his chin as though he had an invisible beard. Did faeries shave? Doubtful. "You need more information. You should speak with a chronicler."

I smiled dryly over the rim of my mug. "A chronicler's the reason I'm in trouble with Kris and your buddy Harrison. I'm pretty sure Simon St. Jerome sent the Titania my way to get her ritual, and we got it from Kris. I kicked his ass for it, and it must've been the straw that broke the camel's back."

"Ah. I see."

"No, you really don't. If I can banish Kris, and that's a big *if*, I'll have to finish the job in the shadow realm. I can't let him go this time. He'll keep coming at me until one of us is dead."

"Didn't you say that people try to kill you all the time?"

The corners of my mouth twitched, and I bit back my response. There's a reason I haven't killed Kris before now. Fighting him was within my ability, but killing an ancient demon takes a lot more power. I'd have to trade a piece of my soul to do it, and I didn't have any more to spare. Summoners trade bits and pieces of our souls away for favors and power, like I'd foolishly traded my sense of taste to win over a boy. Every bit of soul lost is a bit of demon gained, hence my yellow eyes. I'd done enough bad things that I was on the verge of tipping from human to demon. An act like killing Kris would finish me, but I couldn't tell Faust that, so I chose a different truth instead.

"I'm afraid of him. I've kicked his ass a dozen times, but I can't kill him."

His face sobered. "I'll do it," he offered.

I blinked. "You're going to slay my demons for me, babe?" I meant it as a joke, but he didn't laugh.

"Yes," he replied. It was so simple, so matter-of-fact. My dark knight.

I pulled my specs off and rubbed at my eyes, feeling a headache push through the effects of the pink drink. Maybe I'd be lucky and it'd be a fatal brain aneurism, and I wouldn't have to deal with any of this.

"Is that so bad?" he asked softly. His voice was much closer, and I flinched as I opened my eyes and spotted him standing next to me. Pink drink sloshed over the sides of the mug and puddled on the granite top of the island.

"Damn it, I'm going to put a bell on you," I muttered.

"Is it?" he prompted.

"I fight my own battles."

"Technically you don't, because Harvey helps you," he pointed out.

"That's different. And why the sudden change of heart? You haven't said one word about love or romance before. Am I extra attractive now that I'm a damsel in distress?" I reached up and yanked off his glasses, because I was tired of him hiding behind them without a damn good reason. If we were going to have a state of our union address, I wanted to see his uncensored facial expressions.

He peered at me, and I resisted the urge to squirm. "So our time together meant nothing to you?"

I turned my attention back to sipping my drink while my inner monologue screamed, *Lie to him, already!* An irritated growl rumbled up through my chest—yet another demon trait, because normal people don't growl like angry dogs.

"It's not like that," I admitted.

"What *is* it like?" He blinked his pretty black eyelashes at me— I swear, he could star in a mascara commercial—and I sighed.

"It's like a plateful of drama with a side of crazy sauce. I knew from day one that this wasn't going to last because you're going to live forever, so I figured I'd enjoy it until you moved on to the next. It ain't pretty, but that's how it is." I set the mug down and looked for paper towels to clean up the syrupy spill. I suck at meaningful conversation, because I prefer action to talk. My hands itched because I just needed something constructive to *do*.

"You could live forever." I shot him a confused glance, and he clarified, "You could become a necromancer."

"I'm sure Harrison would just *love* that. I'm no necro. I never wanted that." I checked under the sink and found more empty cabinets. "What's the point of having your own place if you don't have anything in it?"

Faust shrugged. "My needs are simple."

"Right. Just so we're clear, exactly what do you *need* from me?"

He glided toward me and pinned me against the cabinets, his arms to either side of my waist. My pulse revved and I swallowed hard. "I want you, Patience."

"That's too vague. Specifics, babe. You want a house? Kids? A Labradoodle? Spit it out."

"What is a Labradoodle?" he asked, frowning.

"A designer dog. Don't dodge the issue."

"I will marry you, if that is what you want."

The floor fell out from under me, or at least it felt that way. I was fairly certain my stomach plummeted down after it, and probably my jaw as well. Maybe I really did hit my head on the way down those stairs and I was still hallucinating all this. My first instinct was to accuse him of not being serious, but this wasn't a joking matter, and his expression was sincere. But still, faeries didn't marry magicians. We're flings, and occasionally baby mommas, but not spouses...wait a minute. My brain ground to a halt.

"You want kids," I accused.

"Of course. I love children."

Sure, I entertained the idea in my daydreams, and it'd been a recurring theme after I turned thirty, but in reality I wasn't ready for that. I planted my palms against his chest and shoved him. "No. No way. I'm way too busy. Not to mention bitchy. And the world's going to end any day now."

"I think you'd make a wonderful mother."

"Well then you must be high. This is crazy...I need a drink. Don't tell me the bar is empty too."

"It is. I'm sorry." Faust took a step back and folded his hands in front of him. "Here, I'll make matters simple. Tell me you don't love me, and I'll drop the subject and never speak of it again."

"That's not fair."

"It seems reasonable to me." He smiled, and I wanted to smack him. Or kiss him. Maybe both. Damn it...I threw my hands up in defeat.

"All right, fine. I love you. But I'm not marrying you or breeding with you, so don't even bother asking. Now, I've had a long day, and the forces of darkness are lining up for the privilege of killing me, so can we just shut up and go to sleep?"

Faust grinned, the very definition of a dazzling smile with his perfect white teeth, and then he pounced on me. I squeaked in surprise, because I was serious about the needing sleep bit. Good thing the pink drink cured what ailed me and I wouldn't have to worry about making my injuries worse.

He pulled me into his arms and kissed me passionately, and when I came up for air it took me a moment to remember what I was going to scold him about. "Exactly what part of *sleep* did you not understand?"

"You can sleep all you want, after I make love to you," he assured me. We were about eye to eye, and I shivered. Ice-blue eyes shouldn't be able to smolder like that, but there was fire in his blood, just as it was in mine. I had a legitimate fear that one night we'd accidentally set the room ablaze and let it burn down around us.

He led me from the room before I could think up a witty retort. The master bedroom was also filled with bland furniture, though the bed was enormous. What's bigger than king-sized? Emperor? Curious, I opened the closet and found it as empty as the kitchen.

"Do you own anything?" I asked, shaking my head as I stood in the doorway.

"As I said, my needs are simple." He slipped his arms around me and kissed the back of my neck. I expected more would follow, but he simply held me until I relaxed against him. I'm not usually the cuddly sort, but it was rather nice.

"Is this the part where you say that all you need is me?" I guessed, and he chuckled.

"Of course."

I shook my head, and then twisted to face him. "Why? I'm sure there are plenty of witches out there who would be happy to swoon over you and have nice, fat babies."

Faust smirked. "I like my women with a little fire in them."

"Ugh. That's a terrible pun."

His grin widened, and then he unbuttoned my blouse with

slow, languid movements. My brow rose. I'd lost a lot of buttons and ruined perfectly good shirts thanks to him, so this was a new development. When the last button was undone, I slipped the blouse off and let it fall to the floor in a puddle of battered, blood-stained silk.

"We don't have all night, you know. I haven't slept in…" I trailed off, frowning. I honestly couldn't remember. The days were beginning to blur together, and I couldn't afford to be that sloppy. "Well, it's been awhile. Probably as long as it's been since I showered. Please tell me there are towels in the bathroom."

I wandered off to find out for myself before he could answer, mostly to give myself some space. There was a strange fluttery feeling in my stomach that I dimly recognized as nervousness. I never get nervous, especially about sex, and I wasn't sure what to make of it. Safest assumption was that my exhausted brain wasn't able to process the sudden appearance of Faust's romantic side.

I flipped the lights on and smirked at the sight of an enormous whirlpool tub. Normally I'm the quick-shower type, but that had fun potential. I could get clean while being dirty at the same time…

Perching on the edge of the tub, I twisted the hot water on full blast—finally something worked in this place. I was beginning to wonder if he owned a model home. Faust sidled closer, appearing curious, and I grabbed hold of the lapels of his jacket and hauled him against me.

"We need to add some casual wear to your wardrobe," I informed him. I tugged the jacket off and let it drop to the floor behind him, and then loosened his tie and tossed it in the vague direction of the door to the bedroom. "Don't get me wrong, I love a man in a suit, but I'm willing to bet your ass would look great in a good pair of jeans."

"I'll agree to wear jeans tomorrow if you wear a skirt," he suggested. "You have lovely legs." He unhooked my bra and threw it on top of his tie.

"No, I have skinny chicken legs."

"Hmm. You are underfed. We must do something about that."

I laughed and deftly unbuttoned his shirt. "Says the man with an empty kitchen. Don't faeries eat?"

"We do, quite a bit. But there's no reason to go to the market when one can do this." A glass of champagne appeared in his hand, and he offered it to me.

"Point taken." Maybe there was something to the idea of having a faerie husband. I took a long drink, and though I couldn't taste whether it was sweet or dry, it was cold and bubbly, which was fine by me. I'd never have to go grocery shopping again...until he traded me in for a younger model. I set the glass aside.

"Babe..." I started, and he interrupted me.

"Liam."

"What?"

"My name is Liam."

An electric jolt of magic surged through me as my inner summoner squeed at learning a faerie's True Name. It's like the summoner Holy Grail. The moment passed and my stomach twisted and knotted into an anxious pretzel.

"No..." I whispered, shaking my head. "I can't know this. Are you *crazy*?"

"I love you. I trust you," he replied. Faust—or Liam, great, another thing to mess with my head—caught my hands in his and held them. He made it sound so simple, but this was the complete opposite of simple. This was life changing.

"And what, you tell all your women your True Name so I now get to be in the club?"

He shook his head. "I've never told anyone before."

Lord and Lady. Steam wafted from the water behind me, yet I was suddenly cold enough for goose bumps to raise the ink of the tattoos that sleeved out my arms. "So why me? Why now?"

"Because you need to know I'm sincere."

"Babe—" I started, and his brow rose. I ground to a halt. Despite my giddiness at knowing it, I couldn't use his True Name. It wasn't right. "I don't doubt that, but you're giving me a loaded gun and expecting me not to pull the trigger. This is the ultimate temptation for a summoner."

"And I trust you," he repeated. He kissed me, and I wanted to strangle him.

"This is blackmail." I poked an accusing finger into his chest. "Emotional blackmail. You think I'll have to stay with you if I know this."

He quirked a brow. "Do you want to leave?"

With an annoyed growl I nudged him back and then turned off the water. I stripped off the rest of my clothes, what little was left. "Shut up and get in," I ordered.

The water was hot enough to boil the average person, but it's difficult to burn someone with as much fire magic as I have. I breathed a happy sigh, and then pounced on Faust after he joined me. I pinned him against the side of the tub and straddled him.

"Okay, listen up. You bullied me into admitting that I love you, and yes, I do. You won that one, so stop pushing. We're going to work this out on my terms, not yours, because I'm the one who is going to get hurt here. I've got years, not millennia. Hell, I might not even have days left now—"

"I won't let anything happen to you." His eyes flashed, which I'd be impressed by except for the fact that mine do that too all the time.

"You want *you* to happen to me," I countered. "You've been in love before, right?"

"Yes," he answered cautiously.

"I haven't. I don't let people get that close. Harvey's the closest thing I have to a friend. All I have is my work, and that's the way it's been since I was old enough to know that for the rest of us lowly mortals, food, clothing and shelter don't appear from thin air. So if you want to start talking hearts and flowers and happily-ever-afters, then we do it at my pace, and on my terms. Understood?"

"Understood."

"Good." I kissed him long and hard until I was sure I'd gotten my point across. "Okay then. Now you can make love to me."

Faust grinned as his arms slid around me, holding me close, and then he kissed me. It was a marathon of a kiss, the kind that leaves you gasping and tingly down to your toes when it's finished. As I caught my breath, his mouth moved to my neck, nipping my earlobe and then nibbling at my throat. I moaned, closing my eyes and enjoying the heat of the water and the feel of his body against mine. He was lean, almost skinny like me, and though he was pale like a vamp, his skin was always slightly hot, also like me. I'd annoyed a few healers who insisted I had a fever, when I was just normally that way.

My eyes blinked open again when his hands moved to cup my breasts. Faust teased my nipples, rolling the peaks between his fingers. A wave of pleasure spiraled through me as I moaned again, and he smiled.

"You make such lovely noises," he commented.

I smirked. "Glad you approve."

He gently nudged me back, and then slipped one hand between my thighs to stroke my sex. I gasped, but then I tried, and failed, to frown sternly at him. "No teasing. We don't have all night."

"You did say I could make love to you," he replied. He dipped two fingers inside me, and I shivered. "I prefer to be thorough."

His fingers slipped in and out, as though accentuating his point. I opened my mouth to argue, but only managed a gasp as another finger joined the first two, and he pumped them in and out. Fast, hard and thorough, each movement brushing my G-spot —I hadn't been a believer in the existence of the G-spot until I met Faust, and he'd converted me. There was something magic about his nimble, dexterous fingers; a millennia or two of practice makes perfect.

"Come for me," he ordered in a low, silken growl. I had just enough thought-processing power left to manage an argument.

"Hey, I said we're doing things at my pace," I pointed out. My voice was more breathy than authoritative, but I got my point across.

"Ah, yes. Of course. Will you please come for me, darling?"

For a moment I marveled at the idea of anyone calling me *darling*, but then I clung to him as I was overwhelmed with a sharp, sudden climax, and I cried out.

"May I also mention that the volume is also quite nice?" Faust commented.

I didn't have the chance to think up a clever retort, because I was too busy moaning as he relentlessly continued to pleasure me. Judging by the volume of my enthusiasm, I'd be apologizing in the morning for traumatizing Harvey. When Faust finally gave me a moment's peace, I tried to catch my breath, but he gripped my hips, maneuvered me into place and slid his cock inside my sex. I would've thought the water and the angle would interfere, but no, he felt amazing as always, and I threw my head back and moaned my approval.

He murmured to me, though I didn't recognize the language. It was lilting and lovely, but not squeaky enough to be faerie, and it didn't sound like any of the languages I spoke. Faust had never been one for endearments before, so I assumed that because I wasn't the *darling* type, he was attempting a different route. His grip tightened until I was sure he'd leave finger-shaped bruises—not that anyone would see them under all my ink—and I gripped the edge of the tub as I rocked my hips to meet his thrusts.

Pleasure rocketed through me and I screamed, and he echoed the sound as he poured himself into me. I clung to him, reveling in every sweet pulse of his cock inside me, and kissed him long and hard.

"Shall we move to the bedroom next?" he suggested when he'd recovered.

"Yes. I'm exhausted."

"I didn't say we were finished," he replied. I blinked at him, surprised, and he grinned. "Like I said, I prefer to be thorough."

He drew the word out, his tone promising all sorts of wicked activities, and I suspected I wasn't going to get to sleep for a long time.

CHAPTER FOUR

I don't do a lot of business with the Order of St. Jerome. My repertoire of spells is wide enough that I don't need things researched often, but I do, on occasion, need more information on targets or my competition. I prefer to work with Dr. Dannaher, the youngest of the three chroniclers in the area, because he doesn't give me the goody two-shoes routine like Michael Black or charge outrageous amounts like Simon St. Jerome. But for this information I needed the best, which meant a trip to see Simon. That was fine by me, because I had a few choice words saved up for him for dragging me into Harrison's crosshairs.

Faust—who I'd decided would stay Faust unless an emergency arose where I needed to use his True Name—bickered with Harvey as I drove to Simon's place in the suburbs. Harvey was displeased at the idea that he'd be a fifth wheel instead of the main male in my life, and I didn't blame him for that. I'd known Harvey much longer than I'd known Faust. He was like family, though that was a dangerous thing for me to think. Even a benign demon like a pooka was still a demon.

I turned down the road leading to Simon's lair, and Faust cursed.

"What's wrong?" I asked.

"Wards," he snapped, and then he and Harvey blinked out of the car. Whoops. I'd been expecting to lose Harvey when I crossed the boundaries of the magical barriers protecting Simon's place, but I didn't know Simon kept faerie wards up. Guess he really hated company. Well, Faust and Harvey could continue their bickering outside the affected area until I talked Simon into letting Faust in. After all, as I'd learned at breakfast that morning, it was in Simon's best interest to hear what he had to say.

Trees lined either side of the crumbling road until I pulled into a clearing. I slowed to a stop and blinked up at the house. Fresh paint, what the fuck? I knew he hadn't moved, because every magician worth their salt in the metropolitan area would've heard about it. Except for librarians, the magical masses don't know about chroniclers or the Order, but if you're important or powerful enough, like me, then you're in the know about all sorts of interesting trivia.

Two cars were parked outside, a sedan and a brand-new SUV. I parked next to them and climbed out of my car. I'd indulged Faust and worn the skirt that he conjured for me—a conservative black pencil skirt with a matching jacket, complete with thigh-high stockings with a sexy seam up the backs and red three-inch heels. It wasn't my normal look, but I could still kill a roomful of people in my high heels without breaking a sweat. At least I'd look good doing it in this ensemble. My heels clicked against new wooden boards as I walked up the steps and onto the porch, and I stopped and rang the doorbell. Another new development, because the door didn't even have a lock before.

The door opened and revealed a dead man, but not the one I was expecting to see. Instead I found Maxwell MacInnes, a librarian who used to own a neutral ground café that I'd been to a few times.

"Huh. I heard you died," I said.

"Rumors of my death are greatly exaggerated," he replied. "You're here to see Mr. St. Jerome?"

"Yes. What's with the home makeover?"

He ushered me inside. "You like it?"

I glanced around the parlor. The place had far more personality than Faust's condo. Warm, inviting, with a touch of class...maybe Faust should hire MacInnes to decorate. "It's nice. Is he up?" I asked. Visiting any bloodsucker during the day was iffy, because they were mostly nocturnal.

"Yes, but..." he trailed off, wincing.

"But?" I prompted.

"He's speaking with the Oberon and Titania."

I barked a bitter laugh. "Oh, goody. The gang's all here."

I knew the rest of the way, so I strode past MacInnes. The stairs to the basement were still a bit rickety, but I didn't turn an ankle in my killer shoes on the way down. New appliances huddled in the corner of the room, another nice update, and the door to the library was open. It jutted out of the cinderblock wall looking less-than-secret, and my brow rose at the sound of raised voices within. Guess no one was having a good week.

Simon was seated at his desk, holding court as usual. The Titania and Oberon, Catherine and Lex Duquesne, stood glaring at him. I didn't like Lex when he was a guardian, and it was worse now that he was Oberon, because now my ability to tell him to go fuck himself was limited by my faerie heritage. My faerie-blooded business was good, and I intended to keep it that way. I'd recently met his lovely bride Catherine, and the jury was still out on how I felt about her. She'd gotten me into trouble, but I found her outcast status interesting, and watching her threaten to cut out the tongue of a witch councilwoman at a "can't we all just get along?" pan-magician meeting was fucking hilarious. I wished I had it on video.

"Please tell me that you idiots aren't coming up with new, fun ways to taunt Zachary Harrison, because I have to tell you, he's really cramping my style," I announced.

The room grew quiet as they turned to look at me. I marched past the Duquesnes and stopped in front of the desk, pointing an accusing finger at Simon. "You son of a bitch. You sent them to my doorstep and told them about my background so I couldn't throw them out. Now I've got Zachary fucking Harrison sending goddamn vampire assassins after me." I whirled and turned my ire at Lex. "And thanks to you two, Kristoff Valkyrie is so pissed at me he punched a hole into this world so he could kick my ass down a flight of stairs and *I don't fucking appreciate it.*"

"Valkyrie is here?" Lex asked.

"Yes, he is. And we can't kill him here, and I don't have a spell big enough to banish him. No one does, because it's not supposed to be possible for him to get here in the first place. Which is why you," I looked back at Simon, "are going to find a spell for me. Free of charge, because you owe me. And if you pull this kind of bull-shit again you and I are going to have a problem."

Simon leaned back in his chair and steepled his fingers. He looked bored, but I knew from experience it took a lot to piss him off. "Are you finished?"

"No." I sat down in one of the empty chairs and primly crossed my legs. "Let Faust in. He's stuck outside your wards, and he's got information for you."

That got a response, though only an irritated crease in his bloodless brow. "You want me to allow a shadowspawn faerie into my home?" Simon asked.

"Yes."

"Faust is all right," Catherine spoke up. "I trust him."

I peered at her. That was unexpected, but they shared a Harrison connection, so it made sense that they'd met. "So do I, for what it's worth."

The chronicler sighed. "Very well." He waved a dismissive hand, and Faust appeared next to my chair. He glanced around the library and bowed in greeting.

"Lovely to see you again so soon, my lady," Faust said to Catherine. "I trust you both are well?"

"Just tell them," I ordered before the conversation dissolved into chitchat.

Faust turned and glared at me from behind his smoky lenses.

Turned out, this was the first test of our new relationship. I had to pry the information out of him over the breakfast table earlier that morning. Last night he'd mentioned that Harrison was gunning for others involved in the Titania debacle, but in the rush I'd forgotten about it, and he didn't tell me who they were until I leaned on him. It didn't bode well. Not that I'd be personally heartbroken if Harrison managed to whack all the members of the local Order of St. Jerome, but they were important, too important to lose due to a fit of temper.

I tapped my wristwatch. "Tick, tock, babe."

"Very well. Against my advice, Zachary has hired several assassins to eliminate Patience, Mr. and Mrs. Michael Black, and yourself, Mr. St. Jerome. I suspect he is also targeting Dr. Dannaher due to his association with your sister Marie, and your sister herself."

Lex's hands clenched into fists and I heard every joint pop. "Why Marie?"

"To hurt you, without hurting *you*. He did promise the Titania that he wouldn't harm you," Faust replied.

"Why the hell didn't you mention this last night?" Lex growled, taking a step toward him. I was on my feet at Faust's side before I even realized it. Huh. Protective instincts. That was new.

"Back off, Duquesne," I warned. "He's doing you a favor."

"Marie is out there right now—"

"In the nice, bright sunshine, so relax," I interrupted. "Call her, if you want."

Lex stalked off, pulling a phone from his pocket. I glanced down and noticed, much to my surprise, that my hands had fired up when I leapt to my sweetie's defense. I shook the flames out and folded my arms across my chest.

"So why didn't you mention it?" Catherine prompted.

"Patience asked me to speak with the Oberon about the threat to her safety, due to the possibility of enacting the favor he owes her. As well as to inform you of Zachary's intentions toward her. I wasn't obligated to mention his other targets."

"Do you know how many individuals young Mr. Harrison has hired, or their names?" Simon asked.

"Five in total, and I don't know their names. They are from the west coast. I believe he may have met them during his trips to Los Angeles."

"I don't believe this. You didn't think you were obligated to mention five vampire assassins?" Catherine asked, throwing her hands up in exasperation. "You were willing to rat him out to protect her. Why not tell us the whole story?"

"What does it matter? You know now. Everybody's fine. No harm, no foul. Can we focus on solving the problem instead of pointing fingers, please?" I said. "Oh, make that both problems. Demon and vampire."

"You only care about saving your own ass," Catherine accused.

"Bitch, please. You think Kris will go home after he kills me? He'll come for you next. You and the little bun in your oven, so don't get self-righteous with me, Titania," I snapped in reply. The blood drained from her face, and she sank into the nearest chair. Good thing she didn't faint, because her husband definitely would've slugged me for that, and I'd have deserved it.

Silence hung in the air like a storm cloud for several tense moments, and then Simon spoke. "You're an Infernus faerie, aren't you?"

I glanced from him to Faust. How the hell had he known that? I barely knew that, and I'd been repeatedly naked with Faust.

"I was," Faust replied. His voice was strained, thick with an emotion I couldn't quite identify—anger? Sadness? The temperature around him leapt about ten degrees, and I knew that was a bad sign. I lit things on fire when I got upset, and I was only part fire faerie.

"Tell me, how is Helen?" Simon asked.

Faust flinched—it was subtle, a slight flicker of movement that I might not have noticed if I wasn't standing next to him, looming over him in my high heels.

"You know Zach's mom?" Catherine asked.

Both men turned to stare at her, and I raised my hand like a grade-school student. "Okay, I'm lost. Is there some sordid, daytime-TV drama going on here that I should know about?"

The corner of Faust's mouth twitched. "An accurate description of most faerie relationships. Yes, my sister Helen is Zachary's mother, and yes, unfortunately Helen and Mr. St. Jerome have met."

Judging by the tension in the air there was something big and ugly hidden within that statement, but Lex returned at that moment. "See, she's fine, isn't she?" I asked, changing the subject.

"She is," he replied. He glared at Faust, his jaw clenched, and I knew we were still in the hot seat.

"Good. Can you find a spell to banish an ancient demon?" I asked.

Simon turned his pale gaze to me, and he no longer looked bored. He looked angry. "I can't help you."

"Can't, or won't?" I replied. The chronicler paused, looking from the Titania, to Faust, and then back to me.

"Magician cooperation, remember?" Catherine said.

Simon frowned. "With all due respect, Titania, I don't believe you understand the magnitude of this situation."

"Take care, chronicler. If you reopen this matter you will not like the results," Faust warned. His tone worried me enough that I reached for his hand in reflex. He glanced up at me, seeming as surprised by the gesture as I was, but he didn't let go.

"This is a lesson in magician history that should not be forgotten," Simon countered icily. "The Infernus clan was responsible for the murder of dozens of innocent magicians. Their crimes were truly evil. Unspeakable."

"For which all of us were punished, even those who had no hand in those crimes, like myself. None of which has any bearing on the fact that there is a demon loose in this world looking to kill Patience, who will surely turn his anger on the Titania and Oberon next. We both owe the Duquesnes our allegiance."

"And yet you were willing to keep silent while assassins went after my sister," Lex accused.

"I'm not certain that Zachary is targeting her. Besides, Miss Marie is more than capable of taking care of herself," Faust replied.

Lex scowled. "But you'd risk it?"

"To see Emily Black dead, yes," Faust snapped.

Things had officially gone over my head. I'd met the woman briefly while doing business with her husband, but nothing appeared important about her to me at the time. Yes, I had heard the rumors that she was a seer in life, but now she was a vampire, and she still managed to seem nice enough. Even conservative by blood drinker standards. There was a kerfluffle over her at our first big magician meeting, where the necros and the chroniclers refused to play nice, but it didn't involve me, so I didn't particularly care about it.

"Why?" the Titania asked.

"Emily uncovered the Infernus's crimes while she was a living seer. They were convicted due to her investigation," Simon said.

"And you're still mad at her about that?" Catherine asked.

"*Mad?*" Faust repeated. He coughed a short, bitter laugh, and I squeezed his hand. "The word is too simple. I don't approve of what my brethren did, and yes, they deserved to be punished for it, but there was no justice in what happened to my clan."

"Justice would have seen you all dead for your crimes," Simon hissed. Damn, he was really pissed. I wondered if he'd lost someone, but I choked down the urge to ask.

"There are things worse than death," Faust replied, his voice low. "I let my temper get the better of me, because an opportunity like this hasn't arisen since we were banished. I won't apologize, not after what I've been through. But don't let *your* temper interfere with the problems at hand."

"I warned Helen not to interfere with my family, and I meant it," Simon said.

"Your *family?*" Faust laughed, and I flinched at the sound. Dropping my hand, he stepped forward and placed his palms on the desktop, leaning forward as he snarled at Simon. "That is amusing, coming from you, Simon Augustus Wroth. Where do you think you inherited the fire in your blood?"

Simon's eyes widened, and I gasped as I realized I knew those eyes. Faust and Simon were related. This really was some crazy soap-opera shit, but that was surprisingly common in magician society due to our small numbers. The chronicler shook his head, probably in shock. I would be. I was really glad that I knew the faerie in my family tree without a doubt.

"That's not your concern," Simon said.

"Isn't it? Would you like me to tell the tale of how I seduced your mother away from her lord husband? Jane was an exceptionally beautiful woman. All that pale, blonde hair—"

With a snarl, Simon launched himself at Faust, diving over the desk as his hands went for my sweetie's throat, and I grabbed the back of Faust's jacket and hauled him out of the way. The Oberon put himself between the two men as I continued to hustle Faust out of reach. He didn't fight me. In fact, he seemed drained. Exhausted.

"That's enough," Lex shouted.

"You're right. It is," I replied. "Fuck this. We'll all probably all be dead by the end of the year anyway. Come on." I nudged Faust toward the door. He stared at Simon, but after a long moment he turned his attention to me and then nodded. Faust turned and started for the exit, and I followed.

"Patience, wait," the Titania called.

I waved half-heartedly in her direction. "Don't worry. I'll see you all in hell."

CHAPTER FIVE

I discovered something new on the drive back to Faust's place. He was quiet and broody and generally angsty, and seeing him be upset made me upset. That'd never happened before. As a cast-iron bitch, my give-a-fuck meter is pretty low where other people's feelings are concerned. Oh, I try to keep my clients happy, but that's out of a desire to see the check clear. But I hated seeing Faust unhappy, and I took that as a sign of how far gone I was over him.

To fill the silence I put my music on loud while I drove and sang along, badly. Harvey was content in the backseat, or at least as content as he was going to get with Faust in the car. The awkward silence continued upon our arrival in the parking garage, during the journey up in the elevator, and into the penthouse. Harvey disappeared into the guest room, and I hesitated as I wondered what to do. I'd offer Faust a drink if there was booze in the bar, or coffee if there was food in the kitchen. I settled on giving him a hug after I took my shoes off.

"You don't have to talk about it if you don't want to," I said. "Your past is your own business. I'm not going to harass you about it."

He smiled. "I appreciate that. I should explain. You'll need to know some of it."

I curled up on the couch—or at least as much as a person can curl up on creaky leather cushions—and watched as he paced in front of the picture windows looking out over Chicago. The building was along the river, and the view was pretty spectacular, even though it was a gray November afternoon.

"I was very different then. After Faerie was formed, it took time before we realized that there would be no more full-blooded children, and longer before we began to accept it. When that happened, we all changed. Our marriages and our alliances dissolved, and we focused on dallying with magicians to create half-blooded children, in order to preserve what we could of our people. I was..." he trailed off, his brow furrowed.

"A slut?" I suggested.

Faust laughed. "Accurate." He ran a hand through his hair and then pulled off his glasses, setting them on the glass coffee table. "I had many children. For a time, it was wonderful. I love children."

He grinned, and I pointed at him sternly. "We can negotiate kids if I survive the ridiculous amount of people trying to kill me."

"Hmm. Well that's additional motive to keep you safe then," he teased. His smile dimmed, and he sat next to me. Two cups of coffee appeared on the table, and he handed me one. I wrapped my hands around the warmth and sipped at it.

"So Simon was one of your brood?" I asked.

"Yes. His situation was unique. His mother was not a magician, but I pursued her anyway, because I was very taken with her. It was foolish and irresponsible of me. I know now that I endangered Simon by bringing him into a family devoid of magic, but I was certain I could protect him. I looked after him the best I could, and I made sure that he was tutored in magic, but I lost track of him. I had so many children, and humans age so quickly. Like flowers. You bloom and fade."

"You're not helping your argument for a permanent relationship," I pointed out.

"Hmm. Perhaps not. My point is, I had many children, and I lost all of them. I thought Simon died, because I had no idea he'd joined the Order. Officially he'd passed away, and there was even a grave for him in his family's cemetery. I visited it a few times, not knowing he wasn't buried there. I had no reason to doubt it."

I nodded, still sipping my coffee. His cup remained untouched on the table, and he rose and began pacing again.

"After losing so many of my children, I stopped having more. Many faeries did, because we simply became heartbroken. Resigned to our fate. Though there were some, like Helen, who refused to give up. She was obsessed with finding a cure, which became our clan's downfall. She believed we could somehow steal the fertility of living magicians, using their blood to cure our sterility. I disapproved. I told her it was madness and she should stop, but Helen...Helen causes chaos wherever she goes. I should have turned her over to the authorities, but I didn't."

"She's your sister," I said. I was an only child, but I was pretty sure if I had siblings I wouldn't snitch on them to the magic cops. Then again "don't snitch" is practically summoner law.

Faust sighed. "And she is also a self-centered monster who doomed us all. But it was Emily Black who caught us. She was the only one who could, being a seer. It was her testimony that damned us, and then the Council of Three of Great Britain banished us all. There were many who couldn't bear to live with the stigma of being shadowspawn, and they killed themselves. I'd say we lost half that first year. The rest were lost by inches and degrees until..."

He stopped and stared out of the window, though I doubted he was admiring the view. Faust was a lean line of darkness against the gray sky.

"Until?" I prompted.

"Until only Helen and I were left. We are the last of our clan. The council forbade us from attempting to harm Emily Black or her kin. Any actions were met with an instant death sentence, but Zachary is not bound by that rule, and I couldn't resist this opportunity. It's easier to focus my anger on the woman who caught us than on my sister, who is truly responsible. But in a way, I suppose it is my fault. I created Simon, and he created Michael and Emily Black. If not for my own desires, perhaps she wouldn't have been there to catch us. Perhaps Helen would have found a cure."

"We wouldn't be having this conversation if she did. You'd be off boinking some faerie woman, and I wouldn't have been born, because my faerie grandpa also would've been off boinking a faerie woman instead of my summoner grandma," I pointed out. "You can't drown yourself in *what might've beens*. It is what it is."

"Practical as always, my dear."

I smiled. "That's why they pay me the big money. So how long have you known that Simon wasn't dead? Or completely dead, anyway."

"I never saw him during the trial. I heard the name Simon St. Jerome, but had no idea that he was my son, Simon Wroth. Then I spotted him at the Duquesnes' magician meeting. It was like seeing a ghost. I thought for certain that I was mistaken, but Zachary knew his True Name. One of the other councilmen, Vargas I think, had known him before he took the St. Jerome name as his own."

"And you were willing to let the assassins get him to get back at Mrs. Black?"

Faust snorted. "Any son of mine can certainly handle a master necromancer. Simon was remarkably talented in life. I'm sure the centuries have allowed him to learn more than a few new tricks."

"Centuries," I repeated, and then set my coffee down. Fuck me. My honey had a kid older than the country I paid my federal taxes to. If I married Faust, would that make me Simon's step-mom? That had to be the most fucked up thing in the history of ever.

"Okay then. Come here and sit down." I patted the spot next to me on the couch, and he did as ordered. I straddled his lap, and he took off my specs and set them aside before resting his hands on my thighs.

"I do like this skirt," he commented.

"You should, you made it. Now pay attention. You did the right thing by warning them, but they won't thank you for it. You're a bad guy, like me. Blaming us for everything lets the good guys sleep at night. And I'm fine with that. Powers know I don't lose any sleep over the things I've done. I'm not interested in yesterday. I'd rather hear about tomorrow."

Faust smiled and kissed me lightly. "And that is one of the many reasons I love you."

"Ooh, there's more than one reason?" I teased.

"Quite a few. You're special, Patience. Remarkable."

"If you say so. I'm still adjusting to this idea. You never said anything romantic before. Not once." My voice was a little too whiny on that last bit, and I frowned. I wasn't the needy type.

"It would have scared you away if I did, and I couldn't risk that." He caressed my cheek and I blushed, my face burning as though it'd burst into flame.

"So if you'd sworn off kids, how come you want them with me? I mean, I'm a career woman. I don't give off maternal vibes."

"But you don't give off the vibes of a woman who hates children, either," he replied. "Do you?"

"No. I like kids fine enough. I'm not sure I'm good mom material. I'm hardly human anymore."

He shook his head. "You're not that far gone."

"I am. I really am—" I stopped and cleared my throat. He didn't need to know that. I unwound myself from his lap and rose, grabbing his hands and tugging him to his feet. "Enough talking. It's distraction time."

Faust chuckled as I insistently led him into the bedroom, and we stopped talking.

"We can't stay here," I said. Or rather I mumbled it against Faust's naked chest. I envied his skin. There wasn't a mark on him, unlike me, who had enough ink to be a circus freak.

Well, my arms and back were full, but there was still a bit of blank canvas left on my chest and legs.

He brushed a kiss against my hair. "I know. It's safe for now."

"Kris'll find it. I assume that since you're spending all this time with me that Harrison's going to notice you're missing, and he'll figure out something's up."

"He hasn't called for me."

I peered up at him. He'd changed his hairstyle a few weeks ago and grown it out so that it brushed his shoulders, and the sleek black mass of it looked fabulous against the white of his pillow. I was forced to admit that he was prettier than me, but I was strangely okay with that.

"Is that normal? Aren't you his right hand man?" I asked.

"Yes, I am, and it isn't normal," he admitted. "The Titania has been calling me quite frequently, but I am ignoring her."

"Won't that get you into trouble?"

"I am very fond of Catherine, but as a shadowspawn, I am not obligated to obey her. If that matter is serious enough, she will send someone to fetch me."

I glanced at the clock. It was nearly 9 p.m., so there was plenty of time left to get stuff done. "Well, we can deal with the vamps when they show up, but in the meantime we need to figure out what to do with Kris. I'm going to need my books from my place."

He frowned. "You said you didn't have a spell that could do it."

"I don't. I'm going to have to make something up and hope it works."

"Perhaps you should speak to Simon without me present."

"No. It was worth a shot to ask, but we probably don't have that kind of time anyway. Chroniclers don't exactly research at the speed of Google. Can you port us in and out of my place? I'd rather not drive and risk someone seeing us coming."

"Of course. We should wait until morning, to minimize the chance of encountering master necromancers."

I smirked. "Uh-huh. You just want to keep me in bed longer," I accused.

"The thought had crossed my mind…"

"Well if you're going to ravish me again, I'm going to need dinner first, because I'm running on empty." I slid out of bed, and I grabbed my panties and his shirt and slipped them on. I paused and waited for him to follow, and was distracted by the glorious sight of him stretched out, the bed sheet leaving little to the imagination.

"What do you really look like?" I asked, curious.

Faust blinked. "Are you tired of this form?"

"No, no. Trust me, I love your form. I'm just wondering what your natural form is," I explained. "I've spent some time with my Fiera family, so I know what they look like. The wings are nice. I liked the wings you had at the shapeshifter jamboree."

"Those wings aren't natural to my clan, but I do like them. They make a statement."

Did they ever—a sexy, avenging angel statement. "Are you really a redhead?"

"In a manner of speaking. Why do you ask?"

"Simon's a redhead, and you said his mother was blonde."

He winced and sighed, and I had a moment of guilt for bringing it up, but I was honestly curious. If by some miracle we did attempt a permanent relationship, I wanted to know more about him. I shamelessly ogled him as he rose from the bed, and he chuckled.

"I'll show you, if you insist, but I doubt you'll find it as attractive," he said.

"I'm a summoner. You'd be surprised what we find attractive."

Faust snorted with amusement, and then his body shimmered and shifted. His pale skin darkened to a dusty gray, and I placed my palm against his chest. Heat radiated from him, but his skin was dry and almost coarse, reminding me a bit of a pumice stone.

"Careful," he warned. "Don't burn yourself."

I glanced up to retort that it would take a whole lot more heat to burn me, and I started at the sight of his glowing red eyes. They reminded me of my yellow eyes, but with an added intimidation factor. "Neat," I said, impressed.

"Only you would say that, my love," he replied with a smirk.

"The hair is cool too."

Faust had flaming hair. Not red, not bright, but actual fire on the top of his head. I was so glad my hair didn't catch fire when I lit myself up, though it would solve my need for a haircut.

"I don't know what you were worried about. You look fine. I probably wouldn't jump you in this form, because it seems like there would be a chafing problem, but you're not hideous. You look a bit like an incubus I used to know."

"You dallied with an incubus?" he asked, his red eyes wide with shock.

The idea of *dallying* with anyone gave me a moment of pause, but then I shrugged. "Hey, there's a time and a place for everything, and it's called college."

Frowning, he returned to normal, and I kissed him. I meant it to be light and affectionate to prove that I wasn't bothered by his faerie form, but he pulled me into his arms and kissed me breathless. Before he could maneuver me back into bed, I drew away.

"Food first, ravishing second," I reminded.

"Of course. Lead on."

I headed for the kitchen despite the fact that it didn't have any food, and started making mental lists of things we'd need to pick up from my place. Clothes were a priority. Harvey needed the chargers for his gadgets too, so he'd stop charging them in my car. I trailed my fingers over the granite top of the island, and a flicker of movement from the living room caught my attention. My paranoid reflexes kicked in and I dove for cover. A knife whistled by me and the blade sank into an oak cabinet door, but before I was safe a second knife slammed into my chest, an inch above my heart. I hit the floor and screamed.

Vampires. Had to be. Kris didn't use knives, and the Promethean hunters used bullets and tranquilizer darts. Good things vampires burned as easy as anyone else. I pulled the knife out—it hurt like hell, but I'd live. I lit my hands up just in time for the vamp to land atop the island like a giant undead vulture and make a grab for me. I thrust the flames at him as I scrambled out of the way, but nothing caught.

The vamp was a pale bastard in dark clothes—which pretty much summed up the lot of them—with a terrible Steven Segal ponytail. He bared fangs at me, but his eyes widened in surprise as he suddenly sailed back into the main room. Harvey stood on the other side of the island, his spindly ears twitching furiously.

"Good work," I said, and he nodded.

Faust—now fully dressed again—attacked a second vampire in the living room, slashing at him with a flaming sword. That left the vamp Harvey had just thrown to deal with.

"Hold him," I ordered.

Harvey darted forward and grappled the vampire, who seemed very surprised to be attacked by the Invisible Man. My aim was much better with a stationary target to hit, and the vamp went up in flames. It wouldn't hurt Harvey, because he was fireproof. The vampire screeched and struggled, and I kept the blaze going.

Something grabbed me from behind—three vamps, seriously? My suspicion was confirmed as fangs sank into my neck. *Hold him until he's dead,* I ordered Harvey. The vamp pushed his touchy-feely magic at me, and I shrugged it off, reached up and lit his hair on fire. He dropped me, tearing a meaty chunk out of my neck in the process, and I clamped a hand on the wound to hold it together. Between the gash in my neck and the slice in my chest I was losing a lot of blood. Never a good thing in a roomful of vampires—they might start a feeding frenzy like hungry sharks.

I whirled to face my attacker and spotted Zachary Harrison standing behind me, slapping his hair out. Motherfucker. Guess the spoiled shit decided to get his hands dirty for once. I'd make him regret it.

The flames spread and engulfed my entire body to discourage anyone else from grabbing me. Heat licked at my skin and singed off the little bit of clothing I had on, but naked and alive was better than dead and modest. Harrison eyed me, looking for weaknesses, and I flipped him off with my free hand.

"You hardly seem worth fighting over," he said.

"Go fuck yourself, asshole."

Harrison scowled. "Very eloquent."

"Yeah? Well your temper tantrum is real fucking mature. The Titania doesn't love you. Get over it."

My hand was slick and sticky where I held it against my neck. Not good. *Harvey…*

This one is still alive, Mistress, he replied.

Break his neck. That'll slow him down for a while. Wouldn't kill the bastard, but I needed my minion between me and the playboy in case I passed out. I wobbled, and Harrison darted forward. A dark blur collided with him and shoved him back. Faust, my avenging angel.

"Call off your dogs, Zachary. This has gone too far," Faust snapped.

"No."

Faust stepped forward and raised his blazing sword. "I won't allow this. You are making a mistake, and it ends here."

"You're right. Step aside, and I'll end it."

"Bring it, pretty boy," I snapped. I jumped as someone touched my shoulder, but relaxed when I saw Harvey standing behind me.

"Zachary, I don't want to hurt you, but I will," Faust warned. "Stand down."

"Why are you protecting her? I'm your family," Harrison whined. Well, it sounded whiny to me. He probably thought he was being dramatic.

"Because you're behaving like a spoiled child. Patience has done nothing wrong. I love her. If you continue to pursue this, I will kill you."

The vampire growled as he tensed to attack, and Faust leapt forward and punched him with the pommel of his sword and laid him out flat. Good for him. The victory was short-lived, because my legs crumpled and I fell. Too much blood loss.

"Potions. Bag," I stammered. Harvey rushed off to find it, and Faust appeared at my side.

"Douse yourself, my dear, before you set fire to the carpet," he warned. I nodded, and the flames vanished.

"Mistress, the vampires destroyed your potions," Harvey said, my bag slung over his skinless shoulder. Wonderful. No healing potions. Just what I needed.

"I'll take you to a healer." Faust picked me up, and we blinked out of the room. It was cold and dark for a moment, and then we were in an unfamiliar library. "Catherine, I need your help."

I worried for a moment about being bare-ass naked, but when I glanced down I was wearing the same suit Faust had conjured for me that morning. Hot damn, I loved him. I wanted to tell him, but it was hard to form the words—any words, for that matter. My brain warned, *oh shit, poisoned blade,* a second before the convulsions started and I made a sound like a strangled bird.

"Put her down," the Titania ordered. She loomed over me, and I was never so happy to see a witch. They're all healers. Well, she had gotten me into this mess, the least the woman could do was put me back together.

Faust laid me on the floor, and as my limbs flailed I managed to grab his hand and cling to it for dear life, refusing to let go. Catherine knelt on the other side of me and began chanting something. It rhymed, so I assumed it was witch magic.

"What happened?" Lex asked. He stood near my feet, a tower of disapproving authority.

"Zachary bit her," Faust replied. His voice caught, as though he wanted to say more but couldn't. It couldn't be easy for him. He had so little family left, and here he was siding with me instead of his nephew. I squeezed his hand, and he gave me a reassuring smile. "There were two masters with him. I've never seen them before. Patience took a blade to the shoulder, here," he motioned at the wound, "and I think it may have been poisoned."

I agreed, judging by the *omgwtf* pain I was in. A fresh wave of agony coursed through me, and I choked down a scream and turned it into a string of expletives instead.

"Got it," Catherine said. "Give me a little space, please."

"No," I blurted. I wasn't letting him go.

The Titania looked down at me with an expression I couldn't quite peg—surprise maybe, but with a side of sadness. "Okay. You're good. No worries."

I nodded, and my eyes slipped shut as she worked. The shaking subsided, leaving a burn in its wake. Normally I'm not bothered by heat, but this was the sickly warmth of fever and not the familiar comfort of fire. Faust murmured to me as Catherine worked, and he stroked my hair as he held my hand. I faintly heard the Oberon speaking to someone else, but I was too out of it to hear what was going on. All I knew was that it wasn't Harvey. Wherever we were probably had demon wards. Not uncommon in a magician household, but never fun for my minion, who had to wait outside in the cold.

When the fever fog lifted I was lightheaded, but the pain had faded. They helped me sit up, and I opened my eyes to spot Lex standing across the room with Michael and Emily Black. I turned to Faust and blinked at him.

"You have lost your mind," I said.

"Very likely. You needed a healer. Catherine is the only healer I know who isn't on Zachary's payroll," he replied.

"Right. Thanks for the patch job. We'll get out of your hair now," I said to the Titania.

She shook her head. "Wait. We have questions."

"Don't we all. I need to get to my place and pick up some things. Now's a good time, because we know the vamps are at his place."

"But Kris could be at yours," she countered.

"So could the Prometheans. It's a big fucking party. Look, I have wards…that totally won't work against Kris. Damn it all. This fucking sucks," I muttered. Then I squared my shoulders and put on my best don't-give-a-fuck. "If he's there, you can put me back together again after he kicks my ass. Let's go."

Faust helped me to my feet, but the Oberon stormed over and stopped us before we could pop out. "You're staying and answering questions. That's an order."

I snarled "Eat me, Duquesne" before my brain could remind me that I wasn't supposed to sass him. Not that it'd ever stopped me before. Much. Faust snickered before scolding me. I cleared my throat. "Sorry. Look, Harrison never had a problem with me before you dragged me into your drama, and now he's all ripping my damn throat out. So what do you want from me, Duquesne? What?"

"I want to help you," he replied.

I burst into fit of hysterical laughter—not because it was funny, but at the sheer ridiculousness of it all. As a guardian, Alexander Duquesne busted my chops every time I bent a minor summoner law, like he had the stick of justice stuck up his ass. Guardians... then again maybe he'd mellowed now that he was Oberon.

"Yeah. Right. Pull the other one," I said.

He sighed, his hands on his hips while he studied me, all rugged and annoyed. Still a little wobbly, I clung to my sweetie for comfort and balance. I wasn't sure what Duquesne thought he could do for me. His track record against Harrison wasn't so good lately. The soft sound of a gasp pulled my attention away from the Oberon, and I spotted Mrs. Emily Black eyeing us warily.

"Hey, I don't care about who did what to who on some other continent in some other century. We're going to stay in our separate corners and everyone's keeping their hands and magic to themselves, got it?" I warned.

"You love him," she said. I wasn't sure if that was a statement or accusation.

"Yes...and?" I replied.

She frowned, her brow knitting in confusion. For a vampire she was a modest, prim and proper little thing. She looked more like a schoolmarm than a bloodsucker. Of course I looked more like a biker than a businesswoman, so what did I know?

"Wait, what?" Catherine said.

"Yup. Hearts and flowers, the whole nine yards. We're buying a house in Wheaton and a Labradoodle named George." I hugged Faust in a proper embrace to punctuate my point, and he chuckled, rubbing my back comfortingly.

"I'll hold you to that," he murmured.

I winced. "Maybe not Wheaton. Somewhere less conservative. Forest Park, it's near my office." I drew away enough to look from the Titania to Mrs. Black. "Can we get on with whatever it is you want, so my honey and I can move on to our next thrilling fight against the forces of evil?"

"Never figured I'd hear you say that," Lex said.

For a moment I gritted my teeth before any insults could slip out, and then I took a deep, calming breath. "Since October I've banished two, sometimes three demons a day, every day. It's tough, and I'm exhausted, and I haven't been paid a single dime for my work. Instead I've been battered, bruised, mauled, stabbed, a few cracked ribs, a dislocated shoulder—"

Lex held his hands up. "I get the idea."

"And it's not going to let up. It's going to get worse. And worse. Until there's more of them than there are of us, and powers help us all on that day, because it'll be ugly. So exactly how are you going to help me, o Lord Oberon? I take checks."

"We'll figure something out. Can you tell us anything about what Harrison has planned?" he asked.

"Not that we haven't already told you," Faust replied.

"And Kristoff?"

"He's out there. Other than revenge, I don't know what his agenda is," I said. "Mayhem, probably. You're not safe here. Or anywhere, really. Nobody's got a house-sized ward strong enough to keep out an ancient demon. But killing him is on my to-do list, so don't get your panties in a knot. Anything else?"

"Your auras are linked," Mrs. Black said.

I glanced down, expecting to see some sort of magical ooze going on between Faust and I, but there was nothing out of the ordinary. Well, I was covered in blood and without shoes—I suspected Faust liked the concept of heels but not the reality that they made me much taller than him—but nothing strange aside from that.

"What does that mean?" he asked.

"It means that you are soul mates," she explained.

My first reaction was shock, then a momentary giddiness, followed by a great sadness that settled on me like a weight. "Oh no. I'm so sorry."

"Why?" he asked, clearly startled.

I swallowed hard and managed a weak smile. "Tick tock." I tapped my watch for emphasis, and he nodded slowly. Clearing my throat, I blinked behind the shield of my specs. "Okay then... We'll keep you posted. Anything else before we go?"

"Is it true that you are a member of the Infernus clan?" Michael Black asked.

Faust tensed, but he nodded. "I am."

I could see the chronicler winding up with righteous indignation, so I stepped in front of Faust. "Hey, I said separate corners, no fighting. Cut him some slack, there's only the two of them left anyway."

"Two?" Mrs. Black repeated.

"Myself and my sister are the only ones left of my clan," Faust explained.

Her eyes widened, and I swear she paled, which I wouldn't have thought possible for a vampire. "But...there were hundreds of you."

"Five hundred and forty-three."

The number echoed in my ears. Lord and Lady. That was a small town, and they'd all been exiled. He said half of them had committed suicide that first year, and the sheer magnitude of that many deaths sucked the wind right out of me. I hugged him, because I'm sure he needed it, and I whispered, "Let's go."

He blinked us out of the room without another word.

CHAPTER SIX

We popped into my living room, and it looked like a tornado had torn through it. Though a tornado was entirely possible, because this was Illinois after all, I suspected the damage was of the intruder variety. No vamps, hunters or demons popped out of the shadows to attacks us. My wards felt intact, but that didn't mean a thing where Kris was involved, because he could smash through them like a deer through a windshield. There was no sense of a current intruder either, and I called out for Harvey.

"Yes, Mistress?"

"You okay?" I asked. The vamps hadn't seen him to attack him, and he appeared uninjured.

"I am well. You look much better."

"Thanks. It looks clear here to me. What do you think?"

His ears twitched as he glanced around the room. "I agree."

"As do I," Faust spoke up.

"Okay. Harvey, grab whatever you'll need for the next few days, and make it fast."

"Yes, Mistress." He headed off toward his room—yes, unlike most summoners, I spoil my demon with his own room, in addition to all the video games he wants.

I flexed my fingers as I fought the urge to start putting things to rights. The couch and chairs were destroyed, the pillows slashed and foam stuffing scattered across the floor. Glass was shattered in the frame of each of my Van Gogh prints. They weren't worth anything, just high-end poster store copies, but I liked them. They were colorful and interesting and brightened the place up. My TV was smashed, and DVDs were strewn every which way. I felt violated. Nauseous. This was supposed to be my safe haven, my sanctuary from all the terrible things I saw and did while on the clock. Faust hugged me, and I sighed against his shoulder.

"We need to have a conversation," he said.

"I know, but we also need to keep this quick, in case they come back," I said. "Come on, you can help me pack."

"I can provide you with clothes," he offered.

"I noticed. Thanks for dressing me, by the way. I'd rather not flash my naughty bits at the Oberon."

"I'd like to avoid that as well."

I snickered and moved away before he could distract me further. Against my better judgment I peeked into the kitchen and found it equally destroyed. I thought the damage to the living room might've been done during a search, but my dishes were smashed. I doubted anyone could find clues to my whereabouts hidden in the pattern on my china.

With a growl of disgust I headed to my study. The door was open, and I froze as I stepped through. Everything was gone—my spell books, my computer, even my damn mystery novels. The destruction was devastating, but I was more or less prepared for it, and I could deal with that, because I could rebuild. Outright theft of my entire library, on the other hand...

"Aww hell," I muttered. "So much for making my own spell."

Faust stepped past me, headed for my desk. He picked up a piece of paper and read aloud. "Dear Patience, because you have helped yourself to my library so many times, I decided to return the favor. I will see you soon. K.V."

Balling my hands into fists, I let out a stream of expletives that'd make a sailor blush. That *bastard*. I stomped away to my bedroom, which was also in disarray. My stomach twisted, nauseated by the idea that the demon had rifled through my unmentionables. Then again, just because Kris stole my library didn't mean that the vamps and/or the hunters hadn't shown up played a part in the mess. I paused as glass crunched under my conjured shoes, and I looked down at a broken picture frame. A family portrait was obscured by cracks spiderwebbing the glass. I didn't have much in the way of mementoes, so I was pretty young in it—five or six years old, stuffed into an unfortunate pink polka-dotted dress with a matching bow in my hair—and I was surrounded by my parents and my mother's parents. The hunters had killed the lot of them in the recent summoner purge. We weren't close. Not a lot of summoners are what you'd call happy, loving or well-adjusted.

"Is that your family?" Faust asked when he joined me.

I cleared my throat and did the best to shake off the sudden urge to mourn. Now wasn't the time to cry over my relatives, and I still wasn't sure they were deserving of my tears. "Not anymore. Help me flip the bed."

"Why?" He grabbed hold of the end of the mattress, curious.

"I have an emergency stash under the floor."

"Very practical of you."

We hauled the mattress off the bed, followed by the box spring, and leaned the two against my dresser. I hauled a storage container of out-of-season shoes out of the way, and pulled up the floor. A dull gray metal strongbox was hidden beneath the loose boards.

"This was my insurance plan in case I ever needed to split fast and head to a nice, warm country with no extradition laws."

"Should we do that now?" he asked with a wicked grin.

"Tempting, but Kris would find us. Hang on, I need one more thing." I handed him the box and sorted through the chaos of slain pillows and ruined clothing. Finally I found what I was looking for, and I snatched it up.

"Is that a stuffed dog?" Faust asked.

"Yes."

"Is its name George?"

"Maybe."

I hurried out of my room and headed to Harvey's. He'd filled a backpack with what he considered the essentials, and appeared to be having a difficult time deciding between what *Legend of Zelda* game to bring with.

"Come on, we're out of here," I said.

"Very well." He scooped up all of his options and added them to his bag. I handed him my stuffed dog, which was, to be more accurate, a Weimaraner named George. I'd had George since I was a baby, and he was the only object in the world I had an emotional attachment to.

"I want you to look after this for me," I ordered. "Keep it safe."

"I'm honored," Harvey replied. I knew he wasn't teasing. In fact he looked a bit taken aback, because he knew how much the toy meant to me. Everything else in my condo was replaceable. George wasn't. Harvey added George to his collection and zipped the backpack closed.

Faust popped us out of my place before anything leapt out to attack us, and we appeared outside the Drake Hotel. Between his charm, and a fake ID with matching credit cards from my stash, we checked into adjoining suites, and Harvey and I covered the rooms in wards. Afterward Harvey disappeared into his suite—again, I spoil my demon, and I didn't want him to complain about overhearing any sexy fun time between Faust and me—I ordered room service.

"I could create food," Faust offered, and I shook my head.

"Normal people order room service. We're trying to appear normal here. Then again, normal people would have luggage." I plopped down on the sofa, and a set of luggage appeared in the room. I laughed and smiled. "Very nice."

"I did promise to provide you with clothing." Sitting beside me, he took one of my hands in his and studied it, as though looking for some sort of magicky connection between us. Soul mates. Ain't that a kick in the head?

"I'm sorry," I apologized again. "The higher powers really are dicks for matching you with someone with the lifespan of a fruit fly."

"It doesn't matter. I love you."

"I love you too, but it *does* matter. It's not fair. You should be matched with another faerie."

"No. I think that would be just as difficult. Most faerie relationships no longer last." He squeezed my hand and smiled reassuringly. "We will just have to enjoy the time we have together... you're certain you won't consider necromancy?"

I wrinkled my nose. "Necromancy is disgusting. Besides, who would I feed on? Harvey? I don't think so."

"True." He continued to peer down at my hand, tracing his thumb over my knuckles in a very distracting way. "I have had many lovers, but only truly loved very few of them. I didn't expect to fall in love again, and then you gave me this." He withdrew a silver pocket watch from his vest. It swayed back and forth at the end of its chain, glinting in the golden light of the room.

My face heated with a blush. I'd given it to him as a winter solstice present last year. "I don't know why, but I thought of you when I saw it, and I knew I had to buy it for you. It seems silly, buying a watch for a faerie, but..."

"But it was perfect." He smiled, and my heart fluttered. Geez, I really had it bad. He made me flustered and awkward like a teenager. "No one had given me a gift in a very long time. Most people ask things of me. Like Helen and Zachary. They're very needy, but they never ask what I want, say thank you, or offer to do things for me."

"What can I do for you?" I asked, curious.

"Marry me."

I laughed and kissed him. "Tell you what. If I live through this, then you and me have a date with a preacher in Vegas."

He grinned, but it was a hollow promise. My survival was a

really big *if*. The fact that I was still kicking after the rest of the summoner population had been killed was pretty miraculous. My concern must have shown on my face, and Faust pulled me to him and held me.

"Everything will be all right," he assured me. I doubted that, but it was nice to hear just the same. "I have so little left. I won't lose you too."

Guilt threatened to swamp me—he was guaranteed to lose me if I killed Kris, but I couldn't tell him that. Instead I forced a weak smile. "We have that in common. You lost your clan. I lost the other summoners. It's us against the world, babe."

"Then we'll just have to look after each other, won't we?"

"Looking after you sounds like a full-time job," I said, and he chuckled.

"The same could be said for you. You're trouble, Patience Roberts."

Truer words had never been said.

CHAPTER SEVEN

Faust stirred and woke me at six in the morning. He didn't seem like an early riser, so I blinked at him with bleary concern.

"What's wrong?" I asked.

He sat up and rubbed his face with his hands. "Simon is calling me."

Huh. Wasn't expecting that one. Honestly I doubted that we'd ever hear from him again.

"You think it's a trap?" I asked.

"Perhaps."

I nodded. "Lemme dress and we'll go."

"You should stay here. Go back to sleep." Faust turned and stroked my hair. It was a perfectly sensible request, so of course I ignored it and got out of bed.

"Nope. We're in this together. You go, I go."

Though he sighed, he nodded in agreement. "Very well." His familiar gray suit appeared around him in a quick blink, ruining my view of his nakedness as he rose. Pity. The glasses reappeared as well, and I detoured from finding clothes long enough to gently remove his specs and slip them into his jacket pocket.

"Your eyes are pretty. Stop hiding them," I insisted.

Faust frowned. "I like my spectacles. They make me look mysterious."

"You're mysterious enough on your own. You don't need accessories to enhance it." I kissed him affectionately, meaning to keep it light and walk away, but he wrapped his arms around me. Clothes appeared on my body—blue jeans, a black silk blouse and black combat boots. No bra, and I wondered if he'd left that detail out on purpose. Then again, I barely have any boobs to speak of, so they don't really get in the way.

"Be ready," he warned, and blinked us out of the room.

We appeared back in the library of Simon St. Jerome, and I tensed for a fight. The Titania and Oberon weren't around to put me in faerie-blooded timeout if I was rude, so that was an improvement. But Mr. and Mrs. Michael Black were there, and that didn't bode well. They stood together to the side of the antique wooden desk and looked vaguely displeased to see us. Mrs. Black gasped softly, and I was willing to bet that she recognized the family resemblance between Faust and Simon's eyes. Now that I knew about their connection, I saw a few more similarities—high cheekbones, fair skin, slender hands, and fine, expressive eyebrows.

Faust stepped away from me, folding his hands in front of him. "You called?"

"I located the information you requested," Simon replied. He held out a plain beige folder, and I eyed it suspiciously.

"Free of charge?" I asked.

"In this instance, yes," he replied.

Watching him like a mouse waiting for the cat to pounce, I edged closer and took it. Vamps were fast, even librarian ones, but he remained calm and serene. Simon was usually even-tempered, but now it made me worried. I flipped the folder open and found a few pages covered in Latin. Like any good summoner, Latin is among the languages I speak. There are days I speak it more than I do English.

I quirked a brow at Simon. "Thanks. So it is possible to banish an ancient demon?"

"It hasn't been done in modern times, but we were able to locate a few examples. Mostly legends, but you might be able to draw something useful from them," he said. "I assume you are familiar with the requirements for killing an ancient demon."

"Yup." My stomach somersaulted, but I kept calm as I flipped the folder shut. "Well if that's it, we'll get out of your hair."

"What are the requirements?" Faust asked.

"Don't worry about it, I got it," I assured him. "Tell the Titania we'll let her know when it's done." Or at least Faust would, I amended silently. I'd be stuck in some hell dimension, a newborn demon. I wasn't sure if I'd even remember my previous life; the details were fuzzy on what happened after the change. It was a fate I'd been resigned to for some time. Now it was much more bitter knowing that I had a shot at love and happiness, but wouldn't be able to have it.

"It requires that the summoner sacrifice a piece of his or her soul," Simon said. I wanted to punch through his placid face at that moment.

"Gee, thanks for sharing that with the classroom. Now did you and your buddies want to take another stroll down memory lane, or are we free to go?"

"You can't afford to lose another portion, Miss Roberts," Mrs. Black spoke up. I bet she used her old seer powers to spot that one. My aura was about half and half now, and had been for awhile. It kept me from doing spells I knew would put me over the edge.

"What is wrong with you people? Is it official 'get all up in Patience's business' week? I said I got this." I turned to Faust to demand he port us out, and he was staring at me with an expression I could only assume was horror. My mouth dried up like the Sahara, and I licked my lips.

"Is that true?" Faust asked.

"Can we discuss this somewhere else?" I replied.

"It is true, I assure you," Mrs. Black said.

I pointed at her. "Stop helping."

She frowned, because making others frown is a special talent of mine. "I merely thought you would want to know—"

"Believe me, I know. I was there when I got that way. Yes, if I kill Kris, I'm done. All I can do now is hope I end up as something decent. I really don't want to be a succubus. They're a bunch of heinous bitches."

"Why didn't you say something?" Faust asked.

"Because there aren't any other summoners hanging around to handle Kris, so I'm handling it." I turned away, not liking the hurt in his eyes, and turned my anger at the vampires. "Don't you get it? Every summoner I've ever known—the council, my colleagues, my competition, even my own damn family from my parents to my baby cousins—they're all dead. No one else is coming to help. There is no backup. No cavalry. I've been trying to keep the flood back, but now it's one last battle for me, and then you're all on your fucking own against the horde."

"Surely it can't be *that* bad," Mr. Black said.

"It is. You better make your peace with the higher powers, because if things don't change for the better fast, we'll all be dead within a year." Shoulders squared, I looked at Faust. "Let's go. We have work to do."

He nodded, still clearly flustered, and he took my arm and ported us out before the undead posse could offer any other helpful information that would piss my honey off. We appeared back in the bedroom of our suite, and he grabbed me and pulled me to him. The folder was knocked from my hand, and pieces of paper fluttered to the floor.

"No," he said simply.

"No?" I repeated as my brow rose.

Faust held my face in his hands. "I won't let that happen to you. I swear it."

Magic tingled through my skin at his touch. That was no simple promise, and my eyes widened. "You can't—" I started, and he interrupted me with a kiss. Faust pushed me back until I fell onto the bed, but before he could pin me I grabbed his tie, yanked him down next to me and pinned him instead. "Hey, pay attention. I *have* to do this. I'm the only one who can. It sucks and I'm sorry, but—"

"Let me do it."

My train of thought ground to a screeching, derailed halt. "What?"

"Let me kill him. I've plenty of soul to spare." He grinned, but the smile didn't reach his eyes. This was no laughing matter.

"Not an option. There's no telling what it'll do to you. Introducing that kind of evil into your soul eats you up like a cancer," I warned. I'd seen it happen time and time again in the summoner community, and I had personal experience with the subject. I struggled with it every day—the constant temptation. A million little chances to do the wrong thing. Once you let the darkness in, it's hard to keep it out. Just like after you've made your first kill, the rest that follow are each a little easier.

"I'm sure I can handle it. I am shadowspawn, after all. Quite evil."

He gave me a reassuring smile, and I shook my head.

"You're not evil."

"Of course I am. I've done many bad things. Terrible things," he replied.

The average person might've bought that argument, but not me. I knew better, because I knew the difference between bad and evil. I gently caressed his cheek. He was so damn pretty, and though he was full of wicked mischief, there wasn't an evil bone in his body.

"No, Liam, you're not. You're only evil by association."

Power zinged through me, and he shuddered as though he'd stepped outside on a windy, subzero day, and closed his eyes. "Say it again. No one's said my name in so long."

Though the idea of using his True Name again made me

nervous, I brushed a light kiss across his lips and indulged him. "I love you, Liam. I want to stay with you…"

He opened his eyes and looked up at me imploringly. "Then stay with me. Let me do this for you. For us. You banish him, and I'll kill him."

"No. You'll have to let me go at some point. I'm mortal, remember?" I pointed out. "I'm ready to go out in a blaze of glory. You shouldn't have to endanger yourself like this for a few days more with me."

"Patience, every moment spent with you is worth dying for."

Tears stung my eyes, and I took a slow, steadying breath to fight back the sob clutching my throat. Lord and Lady, that might be the most romantic thing I had ever heard, and I knew he meant every word. There was only one thing I could do.

I lied.

"All right. Let's go back to sleep, and we'll start working on the spell at a more decent hour," I said. Because our field trip hadn't lasted long it was still around about six in the morning, and even creatures of the night have our limits. We'd sleep on it, and I would let him think he won the argument, right up to the end.

His serious expression melted into a mischievous grin as he flipped me beneath him. "I'm sure we can find more entertaining things to do than sleep."

"Don't you ever get tired?" I asked.

"Not often."

Our clothing vanished, but before he could further his wicked plan, I pulled him closer and clung to him. Closing my eyes, I inhaled the familiar scent of him—smoke, he always smelled like smoke, which my inner fire faerie considered fine cologne. Faust was warm, and I enjoyed the simple pleasure of feeling his heart beat and the brush of his breath against my skin. Nothing felt better than being next to him…and nothing would hurt more than losing him.

"Make love to me," I murmured.

"Gladly."

I kept my eyes closed, afraid that if I looked at him I'd burst into tears. He kissed me, and then his lips trailed down the side of my throat, pausing to nibble just beneath my ear before continuing lower. Cupping my breasts, he teased the peaks of my nipples, and I moaned my approval. Exquisite sensations tingled through me, and an eager ache formed beneath my thighs. I needed him inside of me, but as he'd said, Faust preferred to be thorough, and I knew this was only the beginning.

When he was satisfied that I was a whimpering mass of need, he moved his attention down again and lowered his mouth to my sex. Though I was enamored of his talented fingers, they were nothing in comparison to the wickedness of his tongue. My hands tangled in the bed sheets as he licked and sucked, using his mouth and his fingers to pleasure me. I bit back a scream at the first orgasm, but he was relentless, and I gave up attempting to be quiet. I felt wonderful, and I didn't care who heard me.

Amazing sensations flooded me until I was flushed and shaking, and Faust finally drew away. He laid his body over mine and kissed me deeply—I had no idea what I tasted like, but he seemed to enjoy it.

"Look at me," he whispered. I opened my eyes and stared into his as he hovered above me. "I love you, Patience."

"I love you too."

I angled my hips toward him as his cock slid into me, and I shivered at the feeling of completeness. Soul mates...I never would have thought it possible, but as Faust began to move with long, slow thrusts, it made perfect sense. It explained why he stayed when no one else had, why I allowed him closer than anyone else. We needed each other.

Faust murmured endearments, finally in a language I understood, so I was able to enjoy each time he praised my beauty and proclaimed his love and undying devotion. Holding him tightly, I begged him not to stop. I needed more—I needed forever, but that wasn't possible—and I reveled in the pure ecstasy as he increased his pace and rode me fast and hard. After he came, he kissed me slow and thorough, kindling the burn for a second round of lovemaking. He was insatiable, but I didn't argue. I'd be grateful for the little time we had left together, and savor every moment as though it was our last.

CHAPTER EIGHT

While we were busy shopping for ritual components for my big banishing spell, someone burned down my office building. No one was killed, but they could have been. Despite the building's old age, I knew it wasn't a problem with the wiring that started the fire—one of my would-be assassins lit the place up. There was no way of telling if it was Kris, Harrison or the hunters, but my money was on the vampire. It sounded like something he would do. Spoiled brat. Nobody burns down my office but me.

Buying the ingredients strained my checking account—quality eye of newt costs more than you'd think—and composing the spell fried my brain like I creating a last-minute thesis, but I managed it. Faust and Harvey helped with moral support, when they weren't arguing with each other. Harvey liked Faust even less after the discovery of our soul mate status. I didn't understand it—seemed to me it would encourage him to give Faust a break, but if I didn't know better I'd say Harvey was jealous. He shouldn't be, because Harvey was a roommate and business partner, but that was it. Unlike many other summoners, I didn't think it was appropriate to have an intimate relationship with my demon—there are so many men with succubus servants that summoner gatherings can feel like a trip to the strip club. Though it had never occurred to me before, I began wondering if he was lonely. Well, he'd be free of me soon enough. Our contract would end when I ceased to be human, and he could find himself a pooka girlfriend.

Though Harrison's undead assassins had already hit Faust's condo, we decided to do the ritual there. It was unlikely that the vampires would return, the hunters didn't know where Faust lived, and Kris hadn't showed up there yet. We were about to change that, because I needed to summon Kris before I could banish him. And then I needed to banish him before I could kill him. It was going to be a busy night...

"Are you ready to begin?" Faust asked. He stood outside the summoning circle and peered at my handiwork.

"Ready as I'll ever be," I said with a shrug. I didn't want to do this, but it had to be done. A true summoner would've headed for the hills the moment the hunters came calling, but I stayed. I was the idiot trying to plug the holes in the dam just before the flood. My parents would be so disappointed in me.

"I am also prepared," Harvey said.

"Well, then. Shall we?" Faust suggested.

"Right." No time like the present to get us all killed.

The circle was massive, encompassing the entire living area of Faust's condo and even edging into the kitchen. Bigger was often better as far as summoning was concerned. Normally I'd have Harvey outside the border in case the circle failed, ready to tackle our target and prevent its escape, but tonight both Harvey and Faust were in the circle with me. Their job was to keep Kris busy while I cast the banishing spell. A normal banishing spell is a few lines of text and a component or two, but because I needed so much extra power to boot him, this was going to be a long, drawn-out ritual. I prayed that it worked, because we would all die if it didn't. Well, Harvey and I would probably die, Faust might make it.

As always, the first step to creating the circle was summoning the elements—four corners, four elements. I took wind and water, and let Faust have earth and fire, due to this Infernus roots. Now that I understood his background better, I knew he wasn't just a fire faerie, but more like a lava faerie. My Fiera relatives are pure fire, so it was a sign of the growth in our relationship that I'd handed the element over to him.

After the elements were present, I nodded to Harvey at the edge of the circle. He opened a vein in his wrist with one long claw, and dripped a trail of blood as he walked the circumference of the spell. When he returned to his starting point the magic sealed with an audible snap, and the perimeter glowed with white heat.

"Be ready," I warned.

"Always, my love," Faust replied. Harvey made a noise that sounded suspiciously like a snort, but I let him slide. Faust's flaming sword appeared in his hand as I crossed to the center of the circle.

"Let's hope he's listening," I muttered.

I didn't know Kris's True Name, and that made everything more difficult. His common name, *Kristoff Valkyrie,* didn't hold much power, but because he was gunning for me I was counting on the fact that he'd come when I called. A small cast-iron cauldron waited in the circle's center, and I sliced a shallow cut into the palm of my right hand and squeezed three drops of blood into it. I called out Kris's name, and he appeared, right on schedule.

Unfortunately, he brought backup. A half-dozen shadow demon minions surrounded him, armed and armored like pint-sized body-guards. Kris smiled at me, and I shuddered. My bodyguard squad leapt into action and attacked, and I covered myself in a protective layer of flames. Thankfully I'd come prepared and worn one of my fireproof suits. The thing was black, skintight and looked like a wetsuit, but I wouldn't have to run around stark naked while casting the spell. And it made me feel a bit like Emma Peel, so that was an added bonus.

I did my best to ignore the chaos around me as I began the

banishing spell. There were four physical components—one for each element—and I dropped the first two ingredients into the cauldron. One of Kris's demon minions bowled me over before I could add the third. Dagger-like teeth snapped at my face, barely missing the tip of my nose, and I grabbed the bastard and shoved him off me. The armor weighed him down, and I stopped chanting as I grunted with the effort. Luckily he'd been disarmed, and I only had to worry about being attacked with jaws and claws instead of a sword. When he came at me again, I cast a smaller banishing spell, and he popped back to the shadow realm.

My attacker gone, I returned my attention to the big, bad spell, but I noticed that the demon I'd just dealt with was the only minion who'd been booted from the fray. "Banish the little ones," I reminded Faust. Harvey couldn't banish on his own, and Faust was still adjusting to the idea.

"Right." Faust nodded, and I was relieved to see that he was still in one piece as he kept Kris at bay.

"You won't be able to banish me," Kris snarled.

I plopped the third ingredient into the cauldron. "Care to wager on that?"

Kris lunged in my direction, but Faust intercepted him, and I was free to continue the spell. I picked up the chant where I left off, silently praying that it worked, and then added the last component. Magic surged from the cauldron in a potent ring, and the remaining minions disappeared.

"Ha! I knew you couldn't do it," Kris taunted.

"I'm not done," I replied. I plunged my hands into the cauldron, and the flames surrounding me turned black.

It might've been a trick of the light, but I swore Kris paled. Though he feinted in my direction, he turned and tore into Faust, clawing deep gashes into my sweetie's chest, and I screamed as Faust stumbled and fell back. Harvey tackled Kris's legs like a Monster of the Midway, and the demon went down. With a battle cry, I threw myself into the fray and clamped my burning hands around Kris's throat. He struggled and nearly bucked me off, and as I began the final chant, Kris got in one good punch across my jaw. Pain blossomed through my head, but I spat out a mouthful of blood and continued.

When I spoke the final word, the room seemed to pause for a moment, as though holding its breath, and then I was sent flying by a sonic boom that rang my bell and scattered my team. I smacked into the edge of the circle as though the barrier was as solid as a concrete wall, and thudded to the floor.

For a long moment I stared up at the ceiling, cataloging each bump and bruise as it made its presence known, and then Harvey's skinless face hovered above me.

"Mistress, are you all right?" he asked.

"Did it work?" I asked.

"Yes."

"Then I'm fine. Help me up."

Harvey hauled me to my feet, and I looked for Faust. The blast of magic was contained within the circle, so the room outside had survived unscathed. Inside, the floor was scorched and scarred, and I spotted Faust lying near the center. I hurried over and knelt beside him.

"Are you okay?" I asked. He wasn't bleeding, but his shirt and the jacket of his simple gray suit were torn, and slashes were ripped through his pants as though he'd rumbled with a blender. He blinked, his brow furrowed, and then he nodded.

"I'm well. Just a bit startled." He tried a reassuring smile, but it didn't meet his eyes. He looked worried, and something cold and icy fluttered in my stomach.

"Are you sure?"

"Quite." With a grunt he struggled to sit up, and I glared at Harvey until he helped me get Faust upright.

"You don't look well," Harvey commented.

"I just need a bit of fresh air. If you would be so kind as to fetch our coats?" he replied.

Because Millennium Park wasn't far from Faust's condo, we had decided to head to the Cloud Gate on foot. It would cut down on parking-related drama, and our cars were a tad bit conspicuous. No doubt Harrison's assassins were on the lookout for our vehicles. Walking was sure to confuse them, because, from my experience, vampires hated walking anywhere. Too bourgeois, I suppose.

Faust offered his arm and I clung to it, as though we were a couple out for a late stroll. The November night sky was clear, and a waxing moon hung over the city. I love this city; I'd lived in the Chicagoland area all my life, and I was going to miss it. I really hoped I didn't end up as a succubus. Anything but a succubus. Lord and Lady, if I became a succubus and word got out about it, I'd be bound to some slimeball summoner within minutes as his own personal fucktoy for the rest of his life. Talk about a fate worse than death.

"I love you," I blurted. Faust smiled, chasing away my nervous flutters.

"I love you too, Mistress," Harvey chimed in from behind us.

I laughed, though my honey didn't seem to find it funny. I craned my neck to look up and back at my demon. "More than Zelda?" I asked.

Harvey chittered his demon laughter. "Zelda is easier to love. She needs rescuing more than you do."

"Zelda?" Faust asked.

"She's a princess in one of his video games," I explained.

"And my mistress is a self-rescuing princess."

I rather liked that—*Patience Roberts, last summoner standing, self-rescuing princess.* Too bad it was too late for new business cards.

When we arrived at the Bean, I gave Faust and Harvey talismans to port them to the right place in the shadow realm, and donned my own. They were simple antique keys on black silk cords, each attuned to where we needed to go. I had a collection of keys that led to other worlds—or at least I did, until my office burned down. Lucky for us these keys had been left in my car after my last field trip to the shadow realm.

"Let's go," I ordered.

I led my posse through the mirrored center of the Bean, and we stepped into the shadow realm. It's not one of my favorite places to visit, because my inner fire faerie wants to be somewhere hot and bright, and the shadow realm is the complete opposite.

Harvey growled something in elvish that I knew was one of his favorite expletives, and I turned and squinted, nearly blinded by the light coming from Faust.

"Holy shit. For a shadowspawn, you're really beaming goodness and light," I said. "I thought you come here all the time?"

"No, I pass through here all the time. I've never stopped for an extended stay," he corrected.

Well, if I had still needed proof that Faust wasn't evil, the fact that he was about to blind us all would've been it. Even Duquesne, a former guardian, hadn't been this bright, but then again he was mortal. Faust was made of magic—happy, sunshiney magic, apparently.

"Lord and Lady...hold still."

I cast a cloaking spell over Faust, and the light dimmed to where I could look at him again. He seemed nonchalant for a magical lighthouse that had just beckoned to every demon within the realm.

"It's tingly," he said with a frown.

"Well it won't last long. Let's hustle. Kris's castle is that way." I pointed to a looming shadow on the horizon, almost indistinguishable against the twilit sky.

"You neglected to mention that he owned a castle," Faust replied.

I snorted. "I've yet to meet an ancient demon who doesn't. I think it's part of the package."

"And you don't think that three of us storming a castle will be a problem?" he asked.

"No problem. Harvey and I do it all the time. Don't we?"

"Yes, Mistress."

We shared a long look, because we each knew that this would

be the last castle we stormed together, and there was something terribly sad about that.

"May I have the knife now, please?" Faust asked.

Such a polite request for such a dangerous item. I pulled the weapon from my messenger bag and handed it to him, sheath and all. The blade was pure silver, and the hilt was made from hollow dragon bone covered in arcane runes. It was built to kill ancient demons and other incredibly powerful beings by channeling the wielder's soul through it. Faust attached the weapon to his belt, and I squared my shoulders.

"Come on. We don't have all night. *Tempus fugit*."

I'd invaded Kris's home a dozen times, maybe more, for various reasons. Usually we snuck in, occasionally we got caught, and I'd have to kick Kris's ass, but I'd never seen the place on high alert until now. It reminded me a bit of a supermax prison after an escape—searchlights, sirens, frantic armed guards running to and fro. We hunkered down to watch the chaos and debated what to do next.

"Perhaps we should wait for a more opportune moment," Faust suggested.

"No. As soon as he recovers he'll head back to Earth. Can't have that," I said.

"We may not make it to him if we go through that," he argued, and I shrugged.

"True. You could always turn back."

Faust snarled. "I would never abandon you."

"Good. Cover me." I shucked my winter coat and handed my messenger bag to Harvey for safekeeping. Bright orange flames engulfed my body, and they soothed away my fears. I grinned at my boys, and then broke into a run, because sometimes the best plan is just to rush in and slay them all.

The gate was surrounded by Kris's minions. They rushed me

in a wave of pint-sized anger, and I went to work. I'd always been a hands-on kind of girl where combat is involved. Guns jam, bullets miss, blades break, and all of them can be taken from you, so if *you* are the weapon, you can fight through anything. Harvey took up a position at my right and Faust at my left, and we cleaved a steady path through the defenders, up to Kris's front door.

"I bet it's locked," I said.

"Not a problem," Faust replied. He transferred his sword to his off-hand, placed his right palm against the massive doors, and with a shimmer of magic they exploded inward. The doors shattered into smaller pieces and tumbled down the main hallway, bowling over minions like cannonballs.

"I'm impressed. Library's this way," I directed.

The library was Kris's favorite place, so I knew he'd be holed up in there. Unfortunately for us, the guards within the castle were tougher than the ones who'd been standing at the gate, and by the time we emerged into the room I'd earned a spit lip, a black eye and a few cracked ribs. Irritating, but not debilitating. Harvey and Faust appeared similarly bruised, but were still standing.

"Hello, Patience," Kris greeted.

He stood in the center of the room, his shadowy hands folded in front of him as he gazed at us calmly. I paused, suspecting a trap.

"Do you surrender?" Faust asked.

"Of course not, but before you kill me, I am curious. Is my life truly worth your own?"

I stepped closer, and the demon tensed. "You crossed the line, Kris. I can't risk letting you go back."

"Why? So much trouble over one dying world."

"Because it's not dead yet. The magicians know what your demon buddies are up to, and your invasion's off." I sounded far more confident than I felt, because I knew how tenuous the balance was. With me gone, magiciankind's odds were going to be worse unless the other summoners manned up and pitched in to keep the Midwest secure. If the demons found a way in, they'd multiply like cockroaches.

The demon merely smiled in reply—it's never good when the darkness smiles at you—and I growled and tackled him. At least this was part of the plan, because I'd have to beat him down before he could be killed.

"Keep back," I warned my posse. They wanted to help, but they'd either get in my way or accidentally hurt me in the process.

Kris and I rolled and wrestled as we fought for the upper hand, much like old times, but today I wasn't waiting for him to cry uncle. There was a desperate edge to this fight. His teeth and claws ripped into me, and my flames scorched his skin and started small fires on the carpeting and low bookshelves. The demon struck my already sore jaw, and for a moment I was stunned by the pain. He reached for my throat and ripped deep tears into my skin, and I barely managed to pull away before he got a hold of anything. After Harrison had torn a chunk out of my neck I wasn't eager to repeat that experience.

I ignored the blood streaming from the wound as we continued our battle. For the most part I gave as good as I got, until Kris grabbed my left forearm and twisted, and I screamed as the bones snapped. Harvey tackled him, despite having strict orders not to get involved—what was I going to do, fire him? I stumbled away and tried to regroup as I cradled my arm. Of course Harvey had my bag, which had the healing potions in it. Kris shook my minion off, because though Harvey got an A for effort, him attacking Kris was like a guppy taking on a great white shark, and Kris tossed him across the room and turned his attention back to me.

"You can't—" Kris began to taunt, and I punched him in the throat.

He stumbled away, gasping and choking for air, and I used his distraction to sweep his feet out from under him. Snarling and cursing, I leapt on him, and I grabbed a handful of his filmy shadow-hair and banged his head against the floor over and over until he stopped moving.

"Let me finish it," Faust said.

I looked up and met his pretty eyes, and did the thing I'd dreaded since I'd learned his True Name—I used it to control him.

"Liam, don't move. Stay right where you are."

Magic rocketed through me like a rush of turbo-charged adrenaline, and it was a terribly addictive feeling. I would've smiled, if not for the anguish in my lover's eyes. He'd trusted me, and I betrayed him. He knew what I was about to do, and he was powerless to stop it.

I stumbled to my feet, wincing at the pain in my broken arm. At least I only needed one good hand to use the dagger on Kris. I paused in front of Faust—Liam—who was frozen like a marble statue. I'd rehearsed all the things I wanted to say, and I couldn't remember a single word.

"I'm sorry," I started, and then hiccupped a sob. I didn't cry often, because I was of the opinion that tears don't solve anything, but considering that these were my last words as a human I figured a few tears were allowed. "I'm so sorry, babe, but I can't let you do this. I couldn't live with myself if I let you infect your soul on my behalf. You're not evil. But I am." I smiled weakly. "I've had this coming for a while now. That's why it has to be me. I love you, Liam. Maybe we'll meet again in another life."

I pried the knife from his hand and stepped away, and I turned my attention to Harvey. Much to my surprise, Harvey hugged me. "It's been an honor serving you, Mistress. I'll take good care of George for you."

"You've been a good servant, Harv. And a good friend."

He smiled his bucktoothed pooka smile. "I'll never tell a soul."

I smiled and nodded. Harvey would be all right without me. I was too heartbroken to look at Faust again, and I stared down at Kris's lifeless body.

"Well, Kris, I guess I'll see you in hell," I muttered.

I plunged the dagger into his chest, right where his black heart should be, and magic poured through me and into him. He recovered consciousness long enough to scream in agony, and then his body dissolved into an oily puddle on the library floor. Overwhelming pain exploded through me as a cosmic switch flipped in my soul, and the force of it flung me up, up and away. I crashed through several of Kris's towering bookcases, and as the pain consumed me I prayed for a quick death instead of a new life as a demon.

CHAPTER NINE

"She's got wings!"

My fuzzy thoughts seized hold of the word *wings* and I groaned. Lord and Lady, I was a damn succubus. How was that possible? Sure I'd had a few lovers in my time, and I was a fan of sex, but not so much that it made sense for me to become a succubus. Why couldn't I have been transformed into something cool, like a vengeance demon? They were always fun at parties.

"Mistress, can you hear me?"

Frowning, I tried to blink the darkness away. It sounded like Harvey, but not. The voice was too smooth, like he'd gotten hold of a magical cough drop and it cleared up what ailed him. Plus that didn't make any sense. If I was a succubus I shouldn't still be in the shadow realm, because succubae were native to another hell entirely.

"Patience, darling, we can't linger here," Faust warned.

That startled me enough that I finally opened my eyes, and I spotted two figures crouched a few feet away from me. One I recognized as my sweetie, but the other was tall, platinum blond and naked except for a black nylon messenger bag strategically placed in front of his naughty bits. My frown deepened.

"Mistress?" he said.

Then I spotted the ears—the impossibly long, pointed ears. "Harvey?" He nodded. "You're..."

"An elf," he replied with a wide grin. "And you appear to be a faerie."

That was a thing that could not be. To prove him wrong, I looked down at myself. I'd crash landed in an awkward heap at the foot of another bookcase, covered in moldy, ancient texts. My flames were out, but I didn't see any obvious differences in my body. My broken arm had healed, but my hands appeared the same. Of course with my fireproof suit on there wasn't much to see of me other than black fabric. Succubae had cloven feet, and I was relieved to see that mine were still human-shaped.

"Come here, and I'll take us home." Faust held a hand out to me, and though I had no idea what was going on, I trusted him.

I continued to feel strange as I wobbled upright and stumbled over to him. He caught my hands and held them, and the three of us vanished from Kris's library and reappeared in our suite at the Drake.

"Harvey needs clothes," I blurted.

Not much was making sense, but nakedness was an easily solved problem. Plus it was seriously distracting. I'd gotten used to his skinless state, and I'd never thought of the fact that he didn't wear any clothing. Modesty was a human trait, and though I knew he was male, as a demon Harvey didn't have any dangly bits to cover. I didn't want to see if the same was true as an elf.

"Of course." Faust nodded, and a suitcase appeared next to nude-and-improved Harvey. "If you would be so kind as to give us some time alone?"

"Sure. Just keep the volume down for once." Harvey picked up his suitcase and turned to leave for his adjoining suite, mooning us both in the process. Devoted as I was to my honey, I did note that he had a nice ass, and then felt guilty for having looked.

"Why is he not a demon?" I asked.

"I assume it has something to do with your transformation, and the connection between you," Faust replied.

"How so? I'm supposed to be a demon now too."

He took my hand and led me into the bathroom, and I got my first look at my new self in the mirror. I did indeed have wings. Enormous, flaming butterfly wings. Fiera wings, just like my faerie relatives.

"Holy shit!"

I pulled my specs off to get a better look, and instead of glowing yellow eyes, I found that my eyes had returned to their original light green. Curious, I stripped off my suit and discovered that all of my ink was gone. All of my favors, wards and whatnot had vanished, leaving skin as blank as the day I was born.

"This makes no sense," I said, shaking my head.

Faust cleared his throat—judging by his flushed face he must've been distracted by my sudden nakedness—and he unbuttoned his shirt collar. "I think I may know what happened."

"Can I fly with these?" I asked. It was off the subject, but —wings!

"Yes, and I will teach you later, but first, I'll explain what happened, and then you're going to explain why you broke our agreement."

He pointed an accusing finger at me, and I nodded dutifully. Then I leapt on him and kissed him, filled with joy and passion and general gratefulness to be alive and not a demon. He smiled and held me close. I was willing to bet he had previous experience in making out with a girl with wings.

"I love you," I said.

"I love you too. Now pay attention," he scolded. I nodded again, but was then distracted by the realization that my taste buds had probably been cured along with the rest of me.

"Wait! Food!" I gasped. "I bet I can taste food again. Quick, conjure something chocolate. Wait, champagne! And strawberries!" After all, this deserved a celebration, didn't it? I'd always wondered what champagne tasted like.

Though exasperated, he obliged me. Faust conjured a silver plate with two glasses of champagne surrounded by chocolate-covered strawberries, and I descended upon it like a starving woman. The first bite was cold and sweet—pure heaven. While I indulged in the blissfulness of it, he used my distraction to continue his explanation.

"You're my soul mate, and you're faerie blooded. When you sacrificed that bit of soul, you didn't become a demon because there was more faerie in you than human or demon, because of your connection to me."

"And Harvey came along for the ride?" I asked.

"It would appear so. I assume because you didn't become a demon, it altered your connection, and restored him to his elven state."

I'd made the elves unextinct. I wasn't sure how to feel about that...I wondered how Harvey felt about it. He'd still be lonely as before, and I doubted we'd be able to unextinct a female for him, but like faeries, elves could breed with humans. If we didn't keep an eye on him we could have a gaggle of half-elves running around.

Kids...aww, hell.

"So I'm one hundred percent faerie now?"

"Quite."

"But that means we can't have children," I pointed out, though it pained me to do so.

Faust pondered that silently while I eased the pain by gorging on chocolate-covered strawberries. Aside from the sterility problem, this was an amazing gift. It was like being reborn—I'd been given a second chance.

"I think we might be able to," he said when he finally spoke up.

"How?"

His brow rose. "You do know where children come from, don't you?"

I whapped his arm and he grinned mischievously. "That's not what I meant."

"Of course. You're not a born faerie, and you weren't involved in the formation of Faerie, so you shouldn't be affected by the curse," he explained.

"But aren't you affected?"

"I've never had a problem fathering children."

Right...Lord and Lady, I really was going to be Simon St. Jerome's step-mom. *Wrong.* So very wrong. I shuddered at the thought, and forced my mind away from it, concentrating on the giddy idea that I would be able to live happily ever after with my soul mate. As long as the apocalypse didn't happen.

"Can I still use my summoner magic?" I asked.

"Possibly?" he guessed.

Hmm. If I had super-powered warding spells, I could keep the demons out of our territory and not exhaust myself in the process. We'd have to try that later. I leaned close and nuzzled his neck. *Much later...*

"Patience," he said, his tone scolding. "We agreed that I would kill the shadow demon."

"I couldn't let you. I couldn't let you poison your soul like that. You're not evil. I am."

"Not anymore," he pointed out.

"True. So this is what we're going to do. First, you have to teach me how to turn these wings off before I burn the hotel down. Second, I'm going to need a dress. A white dress."

"A white dress?" he repeated, confused.

"Yes. You promised to marry me, remember?" I reminded. "And then I promised that if we lived through this, we'd get married in Vegas. Harvey can be our witness."

Faust grinned. "Then we had best get started."

EPILOGUE

My honey and I popped into the room, and I had to admit that Zachary Harrison's office was much more old-fashioned than I expected. Of course he had many offices, and this one was in his mansion in Oak Brook, one of his few buildings that didn't have a faerie ward around it. Faerie wards were on my list of new least favorite things.

"This place doesn't seem you. Have you thought of redecorating?" I asked.

Harrison's blond head rose as he looked up from his computer screen, and he stared at me. "How did you get in here?"

"Flew," I said, motioning at my wings. Faust snickered.

"Patience?" Harrison's jaw dropped. I was getting that a lot lately.

"That's Auntie Patience to you, buddy."

I held up my left hand and showed off my blingtastic engagement ring and wedding band. They were very sparkly, and sparkly was on my list of new most favorite things. I had a lot of new favorite things. Becoming a faerie had damaged my brain and now my thoughts ran at warp speed, but for the most part it was positive change. I hoped.

Faust approached his nephew's desk. "What my blushing bride

is attempting to say is that Patience and I are soul mates, and now husband and wife, and that makes her your kin. If you don't call off your assassins, you will become a kinslayer."

The vampire scowled. "Is that all?"

"No. I need a new office. You should be able to handle that, being a real estate mogul and all. I'm thinking something with a view of the lake," I suggested, and his scowl deepened.

"I encourage you to leave your other targets alone as well, because we should be focused on fighting our enemies, and not each other," Faust added.

"Right. I've got the wards covered for now, but we still have a hunter problem," I said. With my new faerie superpowers I could maintain the wards with greater ease and banish more demons, but I was still a one-woman army. As long as the Prometheans were out there, all magicians continued to be at risk.

"Your concerns are noted," Harrison said, his voice a low growl. His attention returned to his computer screen as though Faust and I had ceased to exist.

That didn't sound very cooperative. I began eyeing the office for something flammable.

Faust sighed. "You're being stubborn, Zachary."

"That runs in the family," he replied dryly.

"You did agree to be a part of the new pan-magician council. If you continue with your plans you will put that in jeopardy," Faust warned.

The vampire snarled and leapt to his feet, and it startled me enough that I jumped up and hovered thanks to my flaming wings. My sweetie put himself between me and his nephew, though it was unnecessary. I'd been able to kick Harrison's ass as a summoner, I could do it as a faerie.

"I don't care about the council, and I don't care about being a kinslayer. My enemies will pay for what they've done," Harrison said. Anger saturated his voice, and from my unique angle I spotted the gleam of madness in his eyes. Faust had said that Harrison had become unstable. It seemed like an understatement.

"Now, Zachary, I know you don't mean that," Faust scolded. "You'll have to change your plans for Simon St. Jerome, because he is your kin as well."

That sucked the wind right out of the vampire's sails, and he froze.

"I know, right? The holidays are going to be wacky this year," I commented. Faust sighed at me, and I smiled sweetly.

"How is that possible?" Harrison asked.

Faust opened his mouth to explain, but I was faster. "Well, when two people love each other very much—"

"Patience," my sweetie warned, and I stopped. He turned his attention back to Harrison. "That isn't your concern, Zachary. Now, I understand that you're not well, and that you're upset about losing Catherine, but—"

With an inhuman howl of rage Harrison grabbed hold of his desk and threw it at us. The thing was huge and heavy but he chucked it like a pillow. Faust and I dodged in different directions, and the desk splintered into several pieces when it crashed into the wall—it was an impressive display of temper, and I'll admit, I was concerned.

"*Get out*!" he yelled.

I zoomed down, grabbed Faust's collar, and ported us out of the room before the vampire could grab for him next. We reappeared in our hotel suite, our temporary base of operations, and Harvey looked up from his tablet.

"How'd it go?" he asked.

"Poorly," I replied.

"If I'd had more time," Faust began, but I shook my head. I hugged and kissed him, because I could tell that he was distraught over his nephew's behavior.

"I know you want to help him, but he's not listening. He's going to need some major therapy."

Harvey sniffed. "Don't we all?"

"You're not crazy. You're special," I assured him, and he laughed. I was still adjusting to the elven version of Harvey, but I had to admit that his laugh had greatly improved. It had gone from nasally chittering to a deep, masculine chuckle.

"So what next?" Harvey asked.

"Now we visit the Oberon and the Titania to inform them of the change in Patience's condition," Faust replied.

"Do we really have to? Can't we have more honeymoon first?" I asked. We'd spent the weekend in Vegas, which hardly seemed long enough, but someone had to tend to the local wards, and that someone was me. Plus I didn't want to deal with Lex Duquesne, because he'd only find a way to blame me for becoming a faerie, like it was against the law somehow.

"Yes, we have to. We might as well get it over with, and there is no time like the present."

"Can I stay here?" Harvey asked.

"No. If I have to go, you have to go," I argued.

He sighed. "Yes, Mistress."

Technically I wasn't his boss anymore, because I wasn't a summoner and he wasn't a demon, but I knew Harvey wouldn't be comfortable calling me anything else. Just like I'd never be able to call him anything but Harvey, despite the fact that it wasn't his True Name, and he didn't look much like a Harvey anymore.

Faust popped us out of our hotel suite...and right into the library of Simon St. Jerome. I think we were all startled by that, but the Oberon and Titania were apparently having another chat with him, along with Mr. and Mrs. Black and Maxwell MacInnes.

"You know, for a woman who was so desperate to get away from vampires that she took a trip to a hell dimension and back, you really seem to spend a lot of time with the bloodsucker crowd," I commented.

Everyone stared at me slack-jawed. "Patience?" the Oberon hazarded.

"Yup. I have wings now. Wings are cool."

Aside from the giant flaming wings and green eyes, I didn't look that different. I'd replaced most of my ink with new wards and fun things instead of favors. Faust had even added a few lines of text on my back, just above my wings. It was written in faerie, which I didn't speak—yet—but I suspected it translated to "Property of Liam."

I let him explain the story of my transformation—and Harvey's, which was far more interesting in my humble opinion, because un-extincting an elf was a little like creating dinosaurs for *Jurassic Park*. The chroniclers appeared extremely interested, because learning magician history was their job, after all. Mrs. Emily Black seemed smug. Guess she enjoyed being proved right about the soul mates thing.

"And then Zachary Harrison threw a desk at us," I added as he finished.

"He *threw* a *desk* at you?" the Titania replied.

"I did warn you that he is becoming increasingly unstable," Faust said. "It is fortunate that you are no longer staying with him."

"Why were you staying with him?" I asked.

"Hunters hit our place," she explained.

"That seems to be going around lately. Where are you staying now?" I asked.

"The Duquesnes are currently our guests," Mrs. Black spoke up. That explained why the Titania was at their place when Faust brought me to her for healing after my poisoned blade incident. War made strange bedfellows and all. "Where are *you* staying?"

I shrugged, the skin of my back tingling as my wings fluttered. "Technically we're homeless. My place is trashed, his place is trashed. Harrison burned my office down. But faeries travel light, so we're doing okay."

"Have tablet, will travel," Harvey added.

"We just wanted to update you. I'll make sure the demon population stays in check, and we'll keep an eye out for the hunters and keep the hell out of Harrison's way," I said.

"And pray for those who cross his path," Faust added.

I nodded in agreement. I was glad that we were out of the

vampire's line of fire, but I had a sinking feeling that things were about to get ugly as far as he was concerned.

The Oberon snorted. "We can handle Harrison."

"Really? He just threw a desk at us. You would've been gooey guardian paste on the wall," I retorted.

Catherine Duquesne turned green, and I winced. As a newly-wed, I sympathized, because I would've been upset if my honey had been squished by flying furniture.

"How do you suggest we handle young Mr. Harrison?" Simon asked.

"We try to make him go to rehab?" I said. The Titania snorted —guess she was the only one who got the joke. "Harrison is a *you* problem, not a *we* problem. I don't think he'll be stupid enough to come after us again, but if he does, we've got it covered."

Simon folded his hands and eyed us calmly. "Perhaps, in the interest of magician cooperation, we should work together."

"Why does that sound like a trap?" I asked.

"Because it probably is," Harvey replied.

"What do you propose?" Faust asked, ignoring us.

"You could stay here for the time being. Maxwell has been renovating the house upstairs, and there should be room for all of you," Simon offered.

I glanced at Harvey, and was certain that both of our expressions said, *Trap!* Faust and Simon eyed each other silently, and my high-speed faerie brain tried to list all the possible angles. As a chronicler I was sure that Simon would love to dissect both me and Harvey to discover the details of our transformation, but maybe Simon just wanted quality time to get to know his biological father. It seemed too sentimental for the man, but it was a strange, new world that we were living in... Nah. Dissection was more likely.

Faust cocked his head. "At no charge? Free to come and go as we please?"

"Of course. You would be my guests."

"Well there's a concept for a wacky sitcom," I said. Harvey snickered.

"There is strength in numbers. It would be mutually beneficial," Simon pointed out.

Considering we were faced with hunters, vampires, and enough demons to keep me busy until the apocalypse rolled around, he had a point. I turned to my honey, and he nodded.

I shrugged. "Sure, sign us up."

What was the worst that could happen?

Please enjoy the following excerpt for Bad Blood:

The team seldom investigated cemeteries. As they explained it, cemeteries were for the living, not the dead—a place for grieving friends and family to visit and remember their loved ones. I supposed there was some sense in that, because I wouldn't want to hang out in a cemetery if I were a ghost. I'd want to be where I was most comfortable and had fond memories of. Or somewhere fun, like Disney World or Las Vegas.

Sr. Ramos had informed me that Angela's grave was located outside Barcelona. At first I'd assumed that the distance took visiting them off my itinerary, but the team wanted me to go. I'd emailed Piper a translation of the article about Angela's restless spirit, and she replied with an all-caps excited email and dove into the investigation. She loved a challenge, and the boys thanked me for distracting her from endlessly searching baby name sites. I tried explaining that despite their American assumption that all of Europe is tiny and everything is just next door, Madrid and Barcelona are not close and taking the train there and back would eat up a day of my trip, but the team was excited by the possible ratings bump of investigating a location that I had a personal tie to, so off I went.

A local associate who owed Sr. Ramos a favor had provided me with the cemetery's location. There's something poignantly melancholy about cemeteries—the stoic memorials, faded by years of sun, wind and rain. Generations who had passed from memory, with only a date and a name to remind the living of who had come before. Uncovering those forgotten stories had drawn me to study history. My mother claimed that I suffered from an overabundance of busibodiness and had gone into a profession that paid me to crawl around people's attics and uncover their dirty laundry in forgotten diaries and packets of old letters tied together with crumbling string. It was true enough, though to be fair now I also judged whether that dirty laundry was photogenic enough to be broadcast to the world in high definition.

The sculptures in the cemetery creeped me out. Weeping angels and mournful Madonnas guarded the graves, and I shivered and huddled deeper into my hoodie. I should've worn a sweater under it—I was never truly prepared for local weather no matter how much I agonized over weather reports and wardrobe choices.

I probably also should have grabbed an umbrella, judging by the fat gray clouds lumbering in this direction—the rain had followed me from Madrid like a stalker ex. I kept a rain poncho in my bag as a last resort, but it looked dorky and was awkward to wear. I didn't want to be mistaken for a bright yellow ghost trudging among the tombstones.

My canvas shoes were quickly soaked and stained green as I hurried through the damp, unkempt grass toward the spot on the map that promised to contain the graves of my distant relatives. I frowned at a tiny headstone, the timespan between birth and death only a handful of days. My eyes stung and I swallowed hard.

I didn't have children, and I intended to keep it that way. As the eldest of seven, I'd done my share of childcare while looking after my younger siblings. When I moved out I'd vowed that I would never share a bathroom with anyone ever again. My space was mine and mine alone. I could pick up and travel anywhere at a moment's notice, no babysitters, pet sitters or even plant sitters required. My father called me a free spirit, but my mother simply shook her head at my choices and looked forlorn. I kept hoping that once she reached a certain number of grandchildren she'd give up on me, but thus far she was focused on seeing her firstborn properly married.

A winding, overgrown path wove through the plots, and it led me away from the densely packed dead and onto a lane of stately mausoleums. After I passed the crypts, the trees thickened and the path led into unbeaten territory. I was sure I was headed the right way, but I checked my phone to make sure I still had a signal and functional GPS. I was a city dweller, and I didn't trust the outdoors. Who knew what local wildlife could be lurking in there? Creepy Spanish squirrels? Giant, bullfighting insects? I steeled my nerves and walked into the trees.

The path narrowed and was nearly devoured by brush, but I soldiered on. Between my map and my phone I was certain that I was close, but I was so focused on my guides that I must've missed the branch that slammed into my chest and knocked me back.

Stunned, I landed hard on my butt and cursed as the map and my phone both went flying. I scrambled for my phone before the screen shut off, but the map was nowhere to be seen. I rubbed the screen on my jeans to clean the dirt off and I peered at my position. I was almost there—just a few more feet. I'd make a rubbing of the tombstone, take a few pics and hightail it back to my rented car before the rain hit. I stuffed the phone in my pocket and kept both eyes peeled for the branch that had attacked me, but no further plants attempted to assault me.

I emerged into a small garden—or the remains of one. I'd become accustomed to neglected locations in my travels for the team, who seemed to delight in sending me to abandoned, crumbling sites. The grass was overgrown and invaded the stone pathway that ringed the area. Enormous rosebushes had once been penned in by said path but now sprouted in every direction. The lush red roses bloomed bright, their crimson passion almost sacrilegious in the mournful, forgotten setting. A marble angel spread her wings wide in the center of the clearing, sheltering the final resting place of Angela Rodríguez de Mendoza. Vines had grown up around the statue like living restraints, and the statue's surface was smudged with dirt that had been streaked by the recent rain. It almost looked like the angel was crying.

"Whatever you do, don't blink," I whispered.

I flinched at a crack of thunder, and it spurred me into action. I wove my way through the rosebushes toward the base of the statue. Huh. Angela had her own personal shrine. Why wasn't she with the rest of her family? The name and dates were right. I stepped closer and touched the engraved letters. I tried to forget eighteen. At first, senior year had been a blur of high school drama mixed with crushing academic pressure. My parents couldn't afford to send one of us to college, much less all of us, so I worked my ass off to earn every grant and scholarship I could. I got accepted to a Big Ten school. Everything seemed perfect, until one broken condom popped that life like a balloon.

Another rumble of thunder brought me back to the present

and urged me to action. I withdrew the tracing paper from my messenger bag and taped it over the marble slab. Dad would get a kick out of seeing the rubbing, as though I brought a piece of Spain home and included it as part of their anniversary present. A morbid piece, but still cool nonetheless.

"What are you doing?"

I yelped and the piece of charcoal flew from my hand and sailed into a rosebush. I whirled and faced the speaker, and the explanation flew out of my head as I stared at an angry Latin god. My mouth dried and I licked my lips as I tried to remember how to speak words—any words, English or Spanish.

The man stalked toward me, and I stared dumbly at the skintight black cotton T-shirt and the perfect abs silhouetted beneath it. The equally tight black jeans were also a lovely view, but my self-defense reflexes kicked in when he got too close for comfort. Hands raised and feet planted, I shifted into position for a throw, and the movement gave the stranger pause.

"I said, what are you doing?" he demanded. "How did you get here?"

Oh shit. Was he some sort of cemetery security? Was I about to be booked for trespassing? I should've checked with the office before tromping through with Sr. Ramos's friend's map.

"I walked."

"Through the—?" he asked. I considered myself to be fluent in Spanish, but I wasn't familiar with the last work. It sounded a bit like *border*. Maybe I'd crossed a property line.

"I'm sorry. I didn't see a fence. I..." My mouth gaped like a broken ventriloquist dummy as I suddenly realized that I had no idea how to translate *making a rubbing of a tombstone* into Spanish. "For my mother," I finally blurted. "A copy."

He frowned, and another clap of thunder agreed with his disapproval. The wind picked up and I shivered and wished for the cashmere sweater I'd left in my room, or one of the wool coats I'd left at home.

"Why does your mother need a copy of a stranger's tombstone?"

I straightened. "I'm not a stranger. I'm a relative."

The stranger stilled, then quirked one dark, slender brow. "Oh?"

"Yes. I'm compiling a family tree for my parents' anniversary, and—" A flash of lightning interrupted my explanation. A fat raindrop splashed my nose. I swore softly and dug into my bag for the poncho, but then the heavens opened and dumped rain so fast and furious that I could barely see Señor Tightpants's glower.

He grabbed my hand and pulled me after him. I should have protested, because being dragged away by an unknown Spaniard was not safe or smart. Unfortunately my pepper spray was at home in America thanks to the post-9-11 laws that wouldn't let me carry it on the plane, and the rain nearly drowned me when I opened my mouth to argue.

BAD BLOOD is available now wherever books are sold.

ABOUT THE AUTHOR

Robyn Bachar writes romance with swords, sorcery, spaceships and submersibles. Bachar's novels feature action and adventure, danger and suspense, found families and happily ever afters. Her books have finaled twice in the PRISM Contest for Published Authors, twice in the Passionate Plume Contest, and twice in the EPIC eBook Awards.

In 2019, Bachar's sci-fi romance Galactic Cold War trilogy comes to its climactic finale in END TRANSMISSION (May). Her paranormal romance Bad Witch series continues with BAD BLOOD (January) and BLOOD, BOOK AND CANDLE (July), before reaching its final destination in THE BLOODY END (December). In addition, her fantasy romance Just One Spell series continues with THE TIMEFREEZE CURSE (September).

facebook.com/AuthorRobynBachar

twitter.com/RobynBachar

instagram.com/robynbachar

amazon.com/author/robynbachar

bookbub.com/authors/robyn-bachar

goodreads.com/iamtherobyn

ACKNOWLEDGMENTS

Many thanks go out to Brian, Devin, Karrin and Rebecca, who loved this book; to my family, especially my parents, who are my biggest fans (even though my mother is convinced that I killed her in *Blood, Smoke and Mirrors*); and to my critique group, my RWA chapters, and my editor, Suz, who all make me a better author.

And, last but not least, to my fabulous BFF Diana, who took me in when I needed shelter, supported me through some epic badness, and inspires me every day. Thank you.

OTHER TITLES BY ROBYN BACHAR

The Galactic Cold War Trilogy

Relaunch Mission

Contingency Plan

End Transmission

Just One Spell

The Sephra's Tear

The Timefreeze Curse

Bad Witch: The Emily Chronicles

The Importance of Being Emily

Poison in the Blood

Bad Witch

Blood, Smoke and Mirrors

Bloodlines and Broomsticks

Bewitched, Blooded and Bewildered

Blood, Toil and Trouble

Fire in the Blood

Bad Blood

Blood, Book and Candle

The Bloody End

Cy'ren Rising

Nightfall

Morningstar

Sunsinger

This Apocalypse Bites

Bite Me

BAD WITCH GLOSSARY

alchemist: a magician who specializes in brewing potions. The source of the magic is not the ingredients themselves—though they can help add an extra kick—but the alchemist who infuses her own magic into a potion. Alchemists are the most mercenary magicians because their magic is the most marketable.

chronicler: a librarian who has joined the Order of St. Jerome and become a vampire. Chroniclers undergo a ritual that was originally stolen from the necromancers and altered. It stops their aging and places the body in a sort of stasis. Like the original ritual, there is a chance of failure, and the odds of survival are only thirty to forty percent. To survive, chroniclers ingest magic by consuming the blood of living magicians and often take blood as payment for their services. Chroniclers are responsible for recording magician history and archiving spells and magical research. *See also* Order of St. Jerome.

Council of Three: a magician governing body. Every type of magician is monitored/ruled over by a Council of Three, as are faeries. There are levels to councils—regional, national, global, etc.

demon: an entity native to one of the hell realms. Unlike other magical creatures, demons cannot be killed, only banished back to their realm. However, if a magician travels to that realm, he or she can kill the demon there. Physical attacks on people in "haunted" houses are caused by demonic entities (ghosts can't physically interact with their surroundings). Demons come in a variety of shapes and sizes due to the difference in hells—some embody sins or vices, others natural elements like faeries, and some are just outright nightmarish bogeymen.

faerie: one of the magical races formerly native to Earth. Faeries are extremely long-lived, but are not immortal. In many ways they are embodiments of magic, the different clans representing different aspects and elements of it. Faeries left Earth and created their own world after the extinction of the elves, but that act left them damaged as a species, unable to reproduce with each other. A full-blooded faerie has not been born since the formation of their world. Many magicians owe their magic to their faerie heritage.

favor: a magical debt owed to a demon or summoner. Favors are no small matter, and are granted in exchange for powerful magic. A mark representing the favor is tattooed into the skin of the magician who owes it, and the mark disappears once the favor is repaid.

guardian: an enforcer of magical law and order. They work for the higher powers to ensure criminals are apprehended, but councils are responsible for judging guilt or innocence. Guardians can be called on to execute the guilty, if necessary.

hunter: an individual or group who hunts and kills magicians. Some hunters have personal reasons, such as having a family member killed by shapeshifters. Others do it for sport, believing magicians to be challenging prey.

kinslayer: a magician or magical being who has murdered a member of his/her family. Magicians have always been outnumbered by straights, and after the elves became extinct great importance was placed upon preserving the remaining races. Killing other magicians is frowned upon, but it is considered a great crime to kill a member of one's own family. Kinslayers are often socially ostracized by other magicians.

librarian: a magician specializing in history and research.

Because they study a variety of magics, librarians can cast any type of spell. However, when a librarian casts them, these spells are less powerful. Example, a sorcerer's fireball is less like a softball and more like a golf ball if a librarian casts it. Most librarians aspire to serve the Order of St. Jerome. Though few are chosen to become chroniclers, many work as servants or assistants. *See also* chronicler; Order of St. Jerome.

magician: a person with magic in their blood. Most magicians have inherited their magic from faerie relatives, but in the past many humans were born with their own innate magic. This dwindled over time as magic faded from this world. Only people with magic in their blood can cast magic. No amount of equipment or materials will allow a straight to cast magic.

necromancer: a practitioner of death magic. Necromancers specialize in dealing with ghosts, zombies, and other icky dead things. When a magician becomes a necromancer he is apprenticed to a master, and once his training is complete he undergoes a ritual to become a master himself (*see* vampire). This ritual is risky, with a roughly fifty percent chance of failure. Master necros build up bad karma for jamming a spoke in the wheel of life, and when a master dies horrible things happen to his soul.

oathbreaker: a magician known to have broken an official oath. Sworn oaths are taken very seriously in magician society. If a person swears to do something, such as fulfill a quest or take on a sacred responsibility, failure to uphold the oath can result in social ostracism. Oathbreakers are considered untrustworthy, and few people agree to deal with them.

Oberon: an ambassador responsible for overseeing relations between Earth and Faerie (if the position is held by a woman, she is referred to as a *Titania*). An Oberon or Titania maintains balance between faerie and magician society within a region on Earth, ensuring that faeries do not cause too much mischief within that region, and that the local magicians do not abuse their access to Faerie.

Order of St. Jerome: the organization of chroniclers. The order was founded by a group who decided that having immortal librarians to protect magician records and be able to remember stories and events was necessary to maintain a record of magician history. The necromancers were furious that their ritual for creating immortality had been stolen, but a war between the two factions was prevented when the order agreed not to become involved in magician politics. The group has gone through many names over the years, but St. Jerome is the most recent and longest lasting.

seer: a magician who can read auras and receive prophetic visions. Seers are the rarest kind of magician, with only a handful in the entire world. Their visions center around the person they're reading or a traumatic event in an area. Seers are not mediums, and though they can get a feeling for the energy in a house, they don't communicate with the dead—because that's necromancer territory. Seers are particularly adept at locating a person's soul mate.

shadowspawn: a faerie who has been expelled from Faerie for evil acts. Though faeries have a high tolerance for mischief, they do have limits as to the sort of crimes allowed in and outside of Faerie. Faeries convicted of acts of great evil are expelled from Faerie, banished to live on Earth.

shadow realm: a hell dimension. The shadow realm exists in an eternal state of twilight, where the landscape, buildings and demon inhabitants are made of darkness. Vampires and shadowspawn faeries use the shadow realm as a shortcut to travel between places on Earth that are steeped in darkness. *See also* shadowspawn; shadowstep; vampire.

shadowstep: a method of transportation used by master necromancers, chroniclers and shadowspawn faeries. To keep vampires from causing mayhem in other worlds, the higher powers closed the doors to them—except for the hell dimensions. Shadowspawn faeries and vampires brave or foolish enough to make the trip can travel through the shadow realm.

shapeshifter: a magician infected with wild magic and possessing an animal spirit. The most common shifters are canine, with the rest made up of feline, ursine, equine and avian. Shifters coexist with their animal, almost like having a split personality, and can shift into a hybrid animal/human form and the full animal form. Many shifters, particularly predators, revel in their beast, which has led to shifters being considered subhuman by other magicians and even hunted by sorcerers. *See also* wild magic.

sorcerer: a magician specializing in elemental magic typically destructive in nature. Like witches, sorcerers use elemental magic, and tend to focus on one element in particular. In general their magic does not require spoken spells or physical ingredients; large, formal rituals are rare occurrences. Sorcerers are the magicians most likely to become necromancers, as well as being most likely to be kept as a necromancer's pet.

soul mate: a soul's perfect match. Soul mates are not always romantic partners and can be represented in other close relationships, such as best friends. Because souls are reincarnated, a person can meet his or her soul mate in several lives, or none at all. Also, due to free will soul mates are not guaranteed true love or a happily ever after. Seers can be helpful in finding a person's soul mate.

straights: a slang term for nonmagicians. There are many other terms, such as *voids*.

summoner: a magician dealing in summoning, binding, and/or banishing magical entities. Summoners capture and bind their prey, trading magical favors or power in exchange for release. They mainly deal in demons, but with the right information, such as a True Name, they can deal with any living entity—elementals, imps or faeries. Dealing with demons is risky business and wears on a summoner over time. They begin to take on demonic physical traits and may even become demons themselves, at which point they are often pulled into a hell dimension that becomes their new home.

Task Force Prometheus: a secret government project researching magicians and magic; also known as *hunters* or *Methees* (slang).

While looking for terrorists, the government uncovered the hidden society of magicians. A top-secret task force was formed to study magic-users, to find the source of their magic in order to weaponize it.

Titania: an ambassador responsible for overseeing relations between Earth and Faerie (if the position is held by a man, he is referred to as an *Oberon*). An Oberon or Titania maintains balance between faerie and magician society within a region on Earth, ensuring that faeries do not cause too much mischief within that region, and that the local magicians do not abuse their access to Faerie.

True Name: the name of a magician or magical being that has power over that person. In modern society, names aren't given as much weight and a magician's True Name holds little to no power. It is considered rude to use a magician's True Name, especially without permission. The names of older beings, such as demons, faeries and vampires, can still hold power and be used against them. Faeries in particular guard their True Names jealously and go by a number of pseudonyms.

vampire: a slang term for a master necromancer or chronicler. *Vampire* is considered rude by many older master necros and chroniclers. They do, however, share some traits with the popular vampire myth. They must feed on the blood of living magicians—specifically on the magic within the blood—to maintain their existence. Most keep spouses, partners, or "pets" as blood sources. It is extremely rare for a vampire to kill during feeding (when you're done milking the cow, you don't slaughter it).

wild magic: a form of magic originating from an animal, known to be unpredictable. Most magicians consider shapeshifters to be *infected* with wild magic. This magic imbues its host with the spirit of the animal it originated from, and it also interferes with the host's original magic. Most magicians fear being infected with wild magic.

witch: a magician specializing in elemental magic, focused on healing and self-defense. Witches have a strict policy of doing no harm with their magic, which makes them unique among other magicians. Witches like ritual with their magic, using elaborate spells that require special tools, spoken words and physical ingredients.

www.ingramcontent.com/pod-product-compliance
Lightning Source LLC
Chambersburg PA
CBHW071130100726
47908CB00008B/2557